Art of the Genre represents a huge shared world called The Nameless Realms, a place that spans 13 Ages of Man. Each category of fiction in this world has its own specialized medallion that is 'active' in the upper right corner of each book, thus allowing you to easily tell what specific genre you're purchasing. In the case of The Cursed Legion, you're about to enter an age of Adventure Fantasy, so the medallion you see above is the symbol for all books in that field.

THE CURSED LEGION

SCOTT TAYLOR

Illustrated by
JEFF EASLEY

The Cursed Legion
Copyright © 2012 Art of the Genre

Printed and bound in the United States of America 9 8 7 6 5 4 3 2 1

First edition: April 2012

ISBN: 978-0-9853328-0-8

Cover and Interior Illustrations: Jeff Easley
Continuity Doctor: Katie Redding
Graphic Design: Jeff Laubenstein
Book Design: John Woolley
Cartography and Map: Alyssa Faden
Writing Instructor: Terri-Lynne DeFino
Sounding Board: John O'Neill

Art of the Genre
217 Palos Verdes Blvd,
#217 Redondo Beach,
CA 90277

artofthegenre.myshopify.com

Ordering Information:
For details, contact the publisher at the address above.

I'd like to dedicate this book to my lovely wife of twenty-one years, Portia. Without her support for a clearly insane person this would have never been written.

I'd also like to put in one last thank you to all the fans on Kickstarter who made this dream a reality with their generous donations and to artist Jeff Easley who allowed me to use his talent in a project he really had no idea what would be required of him.

CONTENTS

FOREWORD

Concerning The Cursed Legion: First and foremost I wrote this book to connect with fans of old school adventure fantasy. To achieve this I wanted to place something into the storytelling process that allowed fans a chance to hear directly from the main characters involved. In a way, this harkens back to Meta-gaming, which for all you role-players, I think you get. Anyway, at the beginning of each chapter there is a little aside from the character that controls the point of view for the chapter and it's addressed directly to you, the reader. Certainly, the character has no idea who or what you are, just that they are being observed for whatever reason, so at some points they might be trying to figure out what you are, or place a title to you, and in others they're simply talking because they know someone is listening.

I was always intrigued by what motivated characters in books or what they might be thinking, so I hope you enjoy this aspect of the book, and if not, just skip to the meat of the chapter beneath each opening header.

Secondly, this book was created through the Kickstarter funding platform, so it wouldn't exist without the fans that supported it. I promised them adventure fantasy, something that they could identify with as both fans and players of role-playing games inside that genre. Both myself, and artist Jeff Easley, have gone to great lengths to not only create a fresh new world, but also rekindle some of the magic of illustrated novels so many people enjoyed in the 1980s and even before. I hope we've accomplished our goal, and if you see things in this book that remind you of past published adventures, then you're probably right in your thinking.

ACKNOWLEDGEMENTS

Todd Lockwood, Ian Magee, Eric Garlow, Richard Douglas, Cody "pax" Markle, Marc D. Long, Brandon Haase, Brad Broge, Andrew Maizels, Jaakko Heinonen, Moraya Morningstar, David Anderson, Evaristo Ramos, Baz Stevens, Vergannen, Jason Clark, Adam Thoume, Adam Rains, Stephen D. Sullivan, Scott 'TehMorag' Hellyer

Tyler Walpole, Arturo Albacete, Joe Livesay, Corey Dangel, Michael Zabkar, Brian Everall, Jeff Laubenstein, Lynda & Daniel McCarthy, Justin Larsen, Inga Small, Thuong 'Vu' Pham, Matthew Wood

Leandro Ariel Pezzente, Thom Walls, Stephen, Bob Byrne, Andrew Molloy, Mark Daymude, David (Carthage) Tollen, Andrew and Heleen Durston, Jeff Spangler, Kate Greer, Megan Reigner, Karl Hailperin, Jason G Stockmann, Matthew Gushta, Tony Springer, Ed Stevens, Jon Spence, Chris Baker, Matthias Hoschek, Amanda K. Dawson, Chad White, Rich Strelec

John P. Seibel, Parker, Christopher Thompson, Reto M. Kiefer

Katherine Lim, Jeremy Streeter, Kyle Pinches, Norm Walsh, James Lewis, Nicholas McDonald, Garry Jenkins, Michael M., Luke Gygax, Jeroen Bessems

Danette Akiyama, Jose Alva Jr, Darren Benford-Brown, Jim Alexander, Amos Pons, Dawn Murin, Annette Holguin, Johnathan Bingham, Jason Azze, Jane Ott, RadiantAbyss, Christopher Slye, Caleb Hill, Brent Blackwell, Mary Sutton, Michael P Braun, David DeRocha, Russell Henley, Michael Green, Martyn Warren, Paul Arneil, Banyon Jarvis, Grubnash, David Lars Chamberlain, Bleu Caldwell, M Scholes, Matt LaDue, Adrian Stein, Mikael Olofsson, Chris Sandford, Michael Hurwood, Aaron Wong

Francis & John Morehouse, Peter M. Poulsen, Theo Bingham, Paul Jarman

Benny Hsieh, Doug Rhea, Jason Boyens, Malcolm Lawrenson

The Nameless Realms: The Country of Aflyr

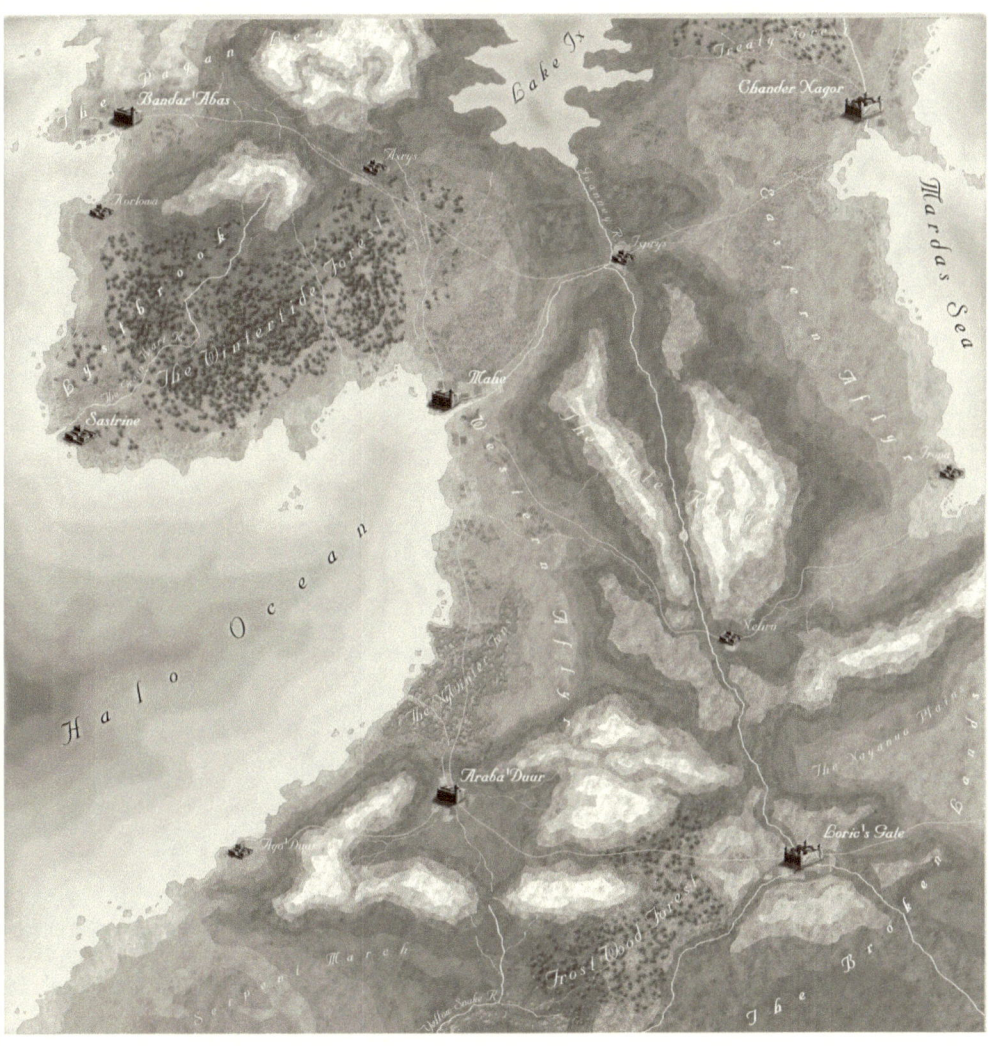

CHAPTER ONE

ERIK

Listen... I know you're there. I'm not sure why, but I'm figuring you're listening, or worse yet watching, so there's really nothing I can do about it but move on, you know? I mean, I'm a bad guy, always have been according to my tutors, but if that makes me important enough for you to take notice, then so be it.

Even now, as I sit here nursing this stale beer I can't help but have thoughts, I mean look at her... seriously, she's gorgeous. If not for the broad-shoulder next to her, I think I'd be forced to make a move, for better or worse. Now I'm not saying I'd force an issue, but I'd take a shot. Does that make me a bad guy because I'd like to bed a woman I've never met? Probably...And most assuredly since my tutors tried hard to teach me respect for women above all else. Still, I can't help but stare.

Do you understand where I'm coming from? Silence... as usual... Well, if you're going to stay around, I suggest you remain silent because I have one of those feelings like something big is about to happen. If there are seats where you are, then pull one up and watch a master at work...

Braxus's laughter exploded, spraying warm beer across Erik's left arm and pants. The pock-faced mercenary wiped tears from rummy

eyes, then ran the back of his hand across the stream of liquid drain-ing from his dripping nose. His scale shirt cast aside across an empty chair, Braxus sat in a greasy undershirt, that hung loosely on his bony frame and was covered in a season's worth of god knows what.

Across from Erik, Malcolm lifted his drink, "Braxus, you can be sure I intend to tell her that when I see her."

Braxus roared again, and Erik flung his wet hand toward the floor, beer droplets puffing up the swath of sawdust beneath his feet. Malcolm, more heavily built and of middling age lifted a tankard with round-knuckled hands. His scars shone white in the lamplight across his weathered face as he turned to look down his long crooked nose at Erik.

"Not in the mood for mirth this evening, my friend?"

Erik smiled and nodded toward the bar, "My mind is on other things."

Both his companions craned their necks in the direction of the lady minstrel, her rich brown hair long and straight with a harsh-banged line across her forehead. She was stretching, just beyond the central fire pit of the hall, slowly lifting up onto her toes and back down again. Beside her a man half-again her size picked at a lute with downcast eyes and an ex-pression that could spoil milk. He was of northern stock, a low elemental fire burning in the corded muscles of his neck and the broad set of his shoulders.

"She's pretty," Braxus said.

Malcolm nodded, "An understatement…"

Heat bloomed at the table, each man's elemental spark coming alight as they watched the girl prepare for her performance.

"Haven't you had enough women this week, Erik?" Malcolm asked.

A barmaid, small-breasted and corset-smashed to look more ample, leaned into the conversation with three more tankards. Her eyes lingered on Erik and he tipped his head before she sauntered away.

"Enough isn't a word I understand," Erik said, his eyes snapping back to the performer.

Braxus took a drink, "It's a curse you must bear…"

"One that will get him killed, but perhaps that's what he wants," Mal-colm added.

Erik kept watching the performer, her voice like honey as she started to sing, the patrons of the bar turning to watch and listen. Captivating the ears and arresting the eyes of the patrons, she sang and swayed like a harem dancer from the Pagan League. She wore leathers, tight about her hips and laced at the groin, a vest and white linen undershirt formed to her chest but her arms were naked save several brass bangles at her wrists.

"What do you make of her?" Malcolm asked.

"She's no commoner, no matter how she dresses, and her companion…"

Braxus interrupted Erik's statement, "Is a bodyguard."

Malcolm took a long drink, his hand falling to the hilt of his dagger, "She might be worth a ransom."

"And you could have her as many times as you like before we turn her over," Braxus said.

Erik shook his head, "That's trouble, and if a defilement bounty gets put on us it means leaving a country we just fled to and without any coin to boot."

"We could play the saviors," Braxus said.

"I like it," Erik began. "And she couldn't be more than seventeen winters which means she's gullible enough to believe anything."

"What about the bodyguard?"

"She's high-born, he's not, which means she probably calls the shots. Besides, they stink of impropriety, so there's a story they're hiding, and that makes them even more vulnerable to us."

"He could be her lover, maybe the man who stole her away from her father's house?" Braxus said.

The two mercenaries looked at Erik who shook his head, "No man who was dipping into that would carry such a frown."

Murmurs of agreement rounded the table.

A fire-haired and short statured little fellow got up from a high seat at the bar and began dancing around the duo, the talismans of a travelling priest bouncing around his small neck.

"I hate Leprechauns…" Malcolm whispered.

"Eldaryn's," Braxus corrected. "You'd better not let the little shit hear you use that name or he'll haunt your coin purse from here to Mahe."

Heat from the newcomer washed over the crowd and Erik wiped his forehead with his beer-damp sleeve. The small priest was thin and resembled the look of a human child of no more than six winters, save for an extended nose, orange mustache, and a heap of blue-orange hair atop his head. Beside him, the singer's hair turned damp with perspiration at his proximity, but she maintained a smile even as her partner glowered at the spinning priest.

The trio finished with a dying falsetto, the Eldaryn taking a bow and the patrons providing a hearty round of applause. Erik stood and walked forward, the priest waving to the crowd as the singer caught her breath.

"Well done," he said.

"Thank you," the Eldaryn replied.

The bodyguard stepped between the girl and Erik, his thigh shoving the Eldaryn out of the conversation.

"Compliments can be paid with coins," the thick man said.

Erik reached for his purse and the bodyguard went for a dagger at his belt. The girl caught her companion's wrist and he paused, dark eyes never leaving Erik's hand. Had the Eldaryn's fire-spark not overwhelmed all, the two men's heat would have been more apparent.

"Pardon my partner," she bowed. "He's a bit overprotective."

Her voice was lilting and bore a tale of tutors and high aristocracy.

"I'm happy to pay coin for your song but I fear your partner might take my hand in the offering," Erik said.

The girl pushed the man aside, a curse escaping his lips as Erik kept his full attention on the singer.

"It would be most kind of you to offer payment, sir," she said.

His fingers unlaced the thongs on a belt-pouch and tricked three silver coins between his knuckles. Heat bloomed suddenly around his hand and as he hissed, pulling it back, the coins fell away into a proffered bag below.

"Coins for the god of tricksters, a most wise offering," the Eldaryn smiled.

The priest looked up with his red irises sparkling and a twitch from his long mustache.

"You smell of wood-smoke and lies," Erik said.

"Compliments will get you everywhere, young man," the Eldaryn bowed. "I'm Ashur Rowani, priest of Bran Bandylegs and player of tricks, at your service. Although, most friends simply call me Ash…"

Erik looked back to the girl, "And you are?"

She stifled a curtsey before pushing a damp lock of hair from her cheek, "I'm Anais Atara."

"A beautiful name," he said.

The bodyguard coughed and the priest flicked the coins from his bag into his vest. Anais blushed, the rose of her cheek flaring the temperature a degree before her partner pulled her away.

"We've wasted enough time, Anais, now let's get some food as the journey will be long tomorrow."

"Journey?" Erik and Ash echoed in unison.

She tried to reply but the brute swept her in front of him as they moved to the bar. When they'd taken seats and ordered drinks, Ash looked up at Erik and whispered, "She's lovely..."

Erik sucked in a breath, nodding, "What brings an Eldaryn to the south shores of Aflyr?"

Ash placed a finger to his nose and gave a wink. "There are powers at play, so says Bandylegs, so I'm here to see a job done."

"And does that job involve getting in my way?"

"We shall see, human, we shall see."

A sigh slipped from Erik's lips as he turned back to his table. Braxus and Malcolm waited there, the two pushing coins back and forth in some attempt to either pay or cheat each other.

"She's a noble for sure," Erik said.

"Does that change the plan?" Malcolm asked.

Braxus looked up, "I hope not, we're almost out of money."

"The bodyguard said something about a journey, so I say we keep our packs at the ready. These roads are dangerous and a lady most certainly needs more protection than a single sword," Erik said.

The barmaid was back with another round and this time whispered in Erik's ear. When she was away he turned back to the bar. Anais, her bodyguard, and a young woodsman in subdued forest greens sat talking. He watched them an hour before the smoke grew thick and the patrons cleared out as the barmaid made a last call. The songstress turned in, and Erik stretched.

Across the room the barmaid slipped away to her rooms and Erik made to follow, Braxus and Malcolm stumbling up to the common room above.

The room smelled of bacon, and the girl's skin held the scents of lust and sweat that both fired Erik's spark and disgusted him. He lay among her rough spun sheets, the ends of straw pricking him in sensitive places as wind clattered the shutter of a single, small window in the chamber.

There was no fire, the adjoining wall to the kitchen heating the room, and the bed served as the only furnishing save a pegged pole where clothes hung.

She'll not be the same, no woman in this backwater plane ever was since I returned from the Archipelago three years ago…

He reached down and ran a finger over her exposed bottom, the girl moaning softly before turning over to gaze at him with dirty-brown eyes.

"Can it be that you wish more?" she asked.

Her voice carried a hint of excitement, and she leaned in to kiss his shoulder. She was a thin thing, small of breast and pale as new milk with a head of sunshine hair dirtied by smoke and grease.

He studied her, the turn of a crooked smile concealing a missing tooth along her upper gum.

"You're beautiful," he whispered.

Her eyes widened then, the smile showing the gap but brightening her features in such a way that she was doubly attractive.

What can you be… fifteen… sixteen winters? Time, or the passing years even for us Humans, hasn't begun to steal your beauty yet in this tattered inn…

"You flatter me…" she replied.

He pulled her close, his mouth finding hers as he tasted the sour edge of sleep residing on her tongue. She kissed him back, pulling herself atop him as their heat burst forth into the cool air of the darkness beyond the bed.

Moaning and biting, she rode him until she cried out and his seed washed unchecked into her womb. He held her close, arms like iron bands around her back as she struggled to breathe.

She nuzzled his neck and he slid his hands up to stroke her hair as the sounds of the waking cook clattered through the thin stone wall. The smell of bread drifted into the chamber, and his mouth watered. Moonlight replaced by the dull glow of a false dawn through a the crack in the window as the girl ran her hands over his chest.

"You'll come to me again tonight? I can make sure you won't have to pay for drink," she said.

"We are leaving as the dawn comes," he whispered against her ear.

She jerked her hand back and stiffened, her disappointment palpable.

"Roma!" the cook called from the hall.

The girl pulled away as a beefy knock struck the door.

"Girl, I'll put you out if you're not in the kitchen before the cock crows."

Roma sat up, her eyes taking him in a last time before she leapt from the bed, ran a damp cloth between her legs from a basin beside the bed, and threw on the serving dress she'd worn the night before.

He watched her all the while, her hands deftly tying her hair up in a leather thong before she moved to the door.

She paused there, a finger resting on her lips, before she turned and dashed back to the bed, kissing him one last time before leaving the room. He thought he heard a sob escape as she disappeared.

Rising from the bed, he dipped the bathing cloth in the icy water and ran it over his body until gooseflesh covered him. He shook his limbs and pulled on his leather breeches, boots, and padded shirt before sliding the coat of scale armor over his shoulders.

Twisting, he adjusted the weight and then buckled on his belt and cloak, a fur-lined helm and traveling-pack slung over his shoulder as he walked to the door. His stomach grumbled when he opened it, the scent of bread having filled the thin hall with its devilishly tantalizing odor but he turned from the kitchen toward the common room.

Today I seek a new sport, one a trifle harder than the common game I had last night...

CHAPTER TWO

RELAN

I walk the land, you know this… you've witnessed my transformation from outcast to warden as I took my apprenticeship with the Hierophant in the Strangler's Deep, and yet this is the first time I've felt your eye truly on me.

What strange twist of fate now draws you to me among the secluded and forgotten hills of the Old Kingdoms? Is there a seed of truth to the Hierophant's worries that his child's mother has finally found him? Do you fear another god coming beneath the boughs of your great trees to take what my master stole in the first place?

These questions do not anger you, I feel that, which makes me question their very strength and validity, and yet there must be some reason you watch over me now. Is this a test? Have you come in judgment of my ability to find that which is sought? I've thrown down Wizards as mighty as gods and yet you come here now to watch my every step along the path to a simple young man?

This is troubling, but I've more important business to deal with than watch over my shoulder for cosmic voyeurs…

The wind slithered up from the south, cold and wet among the tall grass that bled away into western slopes of blue-tinged pines. Relan, cowl drawn up over his lean hawkish face, walked along a stream that cut deep into the clay-rich ground as it wound around the broken stone walls and bare trees of scattered farmsteads, wind howling with the promise of a long winter.

He kept a quarterstaff close, the iron-shod tip testing the ground and a trio of brass firebirds reaching toward the sky above at its head. A cloak of mottled green and grey cloth hung on his thin shoulders, beneath which he wore a shirt of doe-skin covered with a coat of laced wooden rings that shifted like a wicker sea as he walked.

His feet and hands were bare, both darkened with herbal tattoos, the fingers and toes twined with runes that told truths older that the stream running beside him. The path he had been following made a sharp turn and led toward a distant forest. He paused, considering, and then made for the distant trees, whispering words into the chill kiss of wind.

> *"Eyes of the Earth*
> *Guide me through*
> *Keep my steps*
> *Forever true"*

He made his way across a stone fence, drifted among berry thickets dark with the rusty hues of winter, and waded through a sea of gold grasses into a glen still holding mist and frost in its rocky climbs.

The sun, low and pale against the azure sky followed him, glinting off the head of his staff. He walked through streaming golden shafts of light, below trees that whispered secrets with mouthless voices.

Long shadows fell from the west and owls called among the treetops by the time he slowed among a clearing of birch, white and skeletal amid the early winter's grasp. A dwelling of felled saplings bound by grass lay within the pristine thicket, a curtain of bearskin hanging at the only opening.

He approached without pause, his feet making no sound against the yellow grass. Before the threshold a single-bladed axe stood erect in a stump, the metal rusted and the handle wet with evening dew.

Pulling the staff close to his face, he sniffed the wind, a raven calling from the naked branches of a tree nearby.

"Where is he?" Relan whispered.

His words were ripped away by the wind and he closed his eyes, breath settling into a long full rhythm.

"Gone!" the raven cawed.

"To what end?" he asked.

"Gone!" the raven echoed his first cry.

Opening his eyes, he pushed the bearskin aside and stepped beyond the threshold. Inside the hut there were skins piled high, carved wooden trinkets tied with grass, and a few old cooking utensils stashed with a single iron pot.

He took a deep breath.

Even your scent is scant among the fur... you've been gone a while young master...

Outside the sun was drowning in the trees, the south wind stealing the heat of the day and night creatures stirring from their slumber. He settled among the furs, laid his staff beside him, and covered himself.

Tomorrow is another day, with it comes the rebirth of the light and another test of my ability to find the forgotten son of the Hierophant...

The morning began bitterly, with frost coating everything, but the wind died at dawn. As the sun grew strong, it seemed determined to give a final show of power to the coming winter.

Relan took only a meager meal inside the hut. Employing a modicum of magic, his summons of nature's bounty brought little but scant sour berries and late season onions. He ate what was provided and chose no animal sacrifice, although white-tail hare were plentiful about the hut when he emerged into the light.

His path cut south, deeper into the wood that slithered among the rangy hills like moss in the crevasses of a shielding rock. The way was hard and increasingly required the use of his magic to push aside brambles and thickets that would have stayed a mundane man.

Silence followed him, eyes downcast and staff pulling him ever forward as he took rests on the heights and sniffed the wind.

At midday he crested the summit of a large hill, the view of the south spreading out in dusky browns and mustard yellows. A river's course meandered through the distance, and on the horizon scattered plumes of smoke drifted into the sky.

Humanity... a place no son of the wood should find himself...

He looked west, a sea of green and brown stretching as far as the eye could see, broken only occasionally by ancient hills that billowed great towers of steam toward heaven.

You are wise to hide your scent among the stink of men, but I have as many and more tricks than you, young master...

Stepping down from his vantage point, he took the west route among the fading fields and back under the boughs of trees. The wood was old, the trees quiet as stone in his passing, and he attempted no conversation with them as he stole beneath their naked branches.

The Wintertide, forest of the elder days, a barrier to the city-loving humanity that steals down the rivers of Aflyr and plunders the rich waters of the Lystbrook coast...

His bare feet pressed into moss, stone, dry needles, and naturally fallen timber as he walked the game trails that twined through the trees and underbrush. The air smelled of rot and moisture, the busy season of autumn food collecting now replaced by the promise of long months of slumber.

Jumping a rock-lined stream, he walked into the ferns on the far side before pausing when a collection of leaves swayed and chittered around his legs.

"Come out," he demanded.

A small man no more than two feet high with round belly and a robe of brown leaves stepped forth. He stunk of earth, his eyes coal black and his nubby hands set with dirty nails curved for digging.

Damn the luck... an earth sprite...

"What brings a tree-master to the wood?" the sprite asked.

Relan drove his staff into the ground, a flare of heat and white light showering the area. The ferns jostled and rich voices chattered among the low canopy. The lead sprite held his hands over his eyes and bent a knee, his thick mane of black hair pinned with sticks and adorned with moss.

"I've come for my own purpose, sprite. A better question is why do you hinder my passage?" Relan said.

"A fox!" the sprite yelled.

Relan looked around but saw only trembling ferns, the stream flowing by, and the small speaker.

"Of what concern is a fox to me?" he asked.

"He's stealing out winter stores, that's what, and we want you to put a stop to it."

Relan shook his head, "In such matters I stand with neutrality."

The smell of earth grew thick in his nostrils, the little spirit blowing out his belly and standing on his toes. Relan waved the staff before him and the sprite fell back a step but the scent of earth was still strong about him.

"You're intelligent folk and I can't take action against an animal of this forest that is only following its natural instinct," Relan said.

"But it is a damned annoying instinct!" the leader shouted.

"Again, that is not my concern."

The sprite placed a dirty fingernail against his chin, his nose wrinkling. "If we don't get that fox to stop his raids we'll all starve. Does a druid wish that?"

"Again, that is not my concern."

The smell of earth bloomed again, the sprite stomping around in a circle as the ferns chattered once more. When he stopped moving, he turned and said, "Druids are foreign to our forest, perhaps the dog men would like to know you are here? If you wished it, we could cover your tracks."

Lowl... those wolf-headed, and middle-fire hunters will be a problem but I can't intervene in this dispute even it if helped my cause...

Relan sighed, "The Lowl can be a danger, true, but I must continue on my course, be you either help or hindrance to it."

Throwing up his hands the woodland spirit stormed away into the brittle fall overgrowth and swishing ferns. His voice carried insults through the greenery even once he was a good distance from the stream.

"Sprites..." Relan whispered.

From a log not twenty feet away the head of a fox lifted above a fallen tree and stared at him.

"You're welcome," he shouted at it.

With a quick swish of its white and orange tail, the creature leaped down and scurried into the trees.

Relan resumed his walk, a cold mist settling into the wood and he held his staff in a white-knuckle grip as the warmth of its inner fire filled his body.

Threats or no, I must find the Well of Ages to locate the boy... if he's with humans then trouble awaits the entirety of the south... one false step and he will draw on his mother's fury, an untamed squall waiting to be released by her divine spirit...

The forest enveloped him, led him among virgin glens and bowers unseen by the eyes of human or any other elemental first race. This was the seed of the world's power, and through the soles of his feet the earth magic grasped at him, pulling him down, whispering of sweet slumber under the sheltering branches, but he'd heard the call too many times before in the north and he resisted its magical lure.

Night drew a shadow cloak over him. Motes of ghost-light drifted in the darkness while the crooning of night birds cut the silence under the twin moons, first the silver and then the blood.

He moved like a phantom as he skirted the steam vented hills, stole along Lowl trails dangling with rancid territorial markers, and crossed the great valley where ancient covens of xenophobic Aspara sang hauntingly ethereal hymns of fairy magic among the treetop clutches of their unseen villages.

I've passed into the next world, the place where I was reborn even if the forest in which it happened held a different name... Soon I'll find the elder stones and then my course will be set, but I cannot falter... not with so much riding on the outcome.

CHAPTER THREE

ERIK

I feel that you're back... Am I really that interesting? Wait, of course I am, or so the ladies tell me. So what do you think of my newest love interest? No, not the barmaid...

I'm kind of wondering about Anais myself, but I've felt your observation slip away a couple of times and that makes me think either you disapprove of her or there's been something else happening beyond my exploits that draws your interest.

My sister-in-law, on the day of her marriage to my brother, once told me that destiny had a place for me. She was a spooky seer, and yet I brushed her words away, but the next thing I knew I was banished away to the Planar Archipelago for five years of self-preservation training, so perhaps she was as gifted as people thought.

Anyway, if forces are moving about around me, keep an eye on them as well as me, because I might need to be bailed out sometime. That is assuming you've got power to do so and aren't some blundering apprentice with his master's crystal ball.

"Good morning," Erik said.

Anais jumped, and her bodyguard reached for the blade that wasn't at his hip.

"By the gods, you've given me a start!" she said.

Erik smiled and moved around the fence where the two were bridling horses.

"Sorry about that, I was just out for a stretch before my companions and I continued our journey."

The bodyguard took up a position before her as the young woodsman they'd supped with last evening came from the barn with his bow and pack in hand. Anais pressed up on her toes and spoke over her guard's shoulder, "Where do you travel to?"

"Up the coast to Mahe, but I've heard that the fens are dangerous this time of year, the cold weather forcing the inhabitants onto the trade roads looking for easy prey."

Anais looked at her guard, but he shook his head and said, "That's why we've got a guide, he'll be sure we steer clear of such danger."

Erik nodded, "Then you're going to Mahe as well?"

The guard's face fell, a slight touch of color coming to his cheeks. Before he could speak, Anais answered, "Indeed, and I'd say there is safety in numbers."

"You're..." the guard caught himself and choked back a word.

"You're what?" Erik asked.

"You're... right, perhaps a small party is the wiser choice," the guard said.

Erik stepped forward and offered a hand, "Erik of Taux, at your service."

The guard took it, his grip like iron but Erik matched the intensity. "Raziel Grey," he said.

"And I'm Tavalori," the young woodsman offered.

Erik shook his hand as well, all the men sharing a momentary exchange of spark, their fire elements testing the bounds of their new acquaintance. To Erik, Tavalori's element held a strange quiver that chilled his soul.

"I've two other companions," Erik said, "the mercenaries Braxus and Malcolm, both just come from Nehru at the turning of the season."

Anais took Raziel by the arm, "Then we'll have a very merry band."

Raziel's jaw flexed, the heat from him washing over Erik in a wave.

"Not to worry," Erik soothed. "Five swords are better than two."

"As long as they keep them sheathed..." Raziel hissed.

Erik nodded, the voice of Malcolm calling from the front of the inn, "Are we travelling?"

"Indeed," Erik replied.

"Then prepare yourself for an interesting trip, as the Eldaryn has his pony packed and ready as well."

Malcolm's voice held an edge.

Sighing, Erik shook his head and turned away from the warrior and his lady, "At least that means some entertainment during the journey."

When he looked back he said, "Still, we'll cost you no further travel time, for although we have no horses, neither does young Tavalori."

Raziel pulled Anais toward the horses, and as Erik walked back toward the inn, Braxus stepped out from behind a shade tree, dagger in hand.

"I guess I won't be needing this..." the mercenary said.

"No, and I told you that you'd not be *needing* it in any case."

Braxus frowned and sheathed the weapon. "Fine, but that bodyguard will be trouble, you mark my words."

Erik pushed past the man, a seeping aura of heat trailing him as he went.

"How long will it be until we reach Mahe?" Anais asked.

She was riding sidesaddle, and Raziel kept his mount close enough to touch her legs.

Erik removed his helm and ran a gloved hand through his hair before replying, "I'd say no more than five days if this weather holds."

He cast a look to the east, dark clouds looming over the Aflyrian Inlands. Anais followed his eyes for a moment and then returned her focus to him.

"I've heard these coastal marshes don't freeze in the winter," she said.

Erik looked back toward the coast, the cat's tail and marsh grass glowing golden in the late autumn light.

"The western coast of Aflyr is well known for these marshlands. Word as far east as Nehru tells tales of man-eating fish and frogs, bog hags and mist ghosts that lurk inside their depths, but all I've seen so far have been twisting paths and an occasional ground bird. I've been told that the village youths wade through the bogs gigging frogs and netting catfish all winter so they can trade them at market."

She looked to the marsh, asking, "But do they freeze?"

"I can't say, but sailors proclaim the port of Mahe is open to trade year round, which must be a good sign for mild weather," Erik answered.

Anais looked back to him, the shadow of Raziel lurking as he moved his horse forward in an attempt to block their conversation. Erik quickened his pace.

"Are you really from Taux?" Anais asked.

"I've recently come from there, yes."

"I've heard that the New Kingdoms are beautiful." she said.

Erik frowned, the awed intonation of her voice so like the girls he'd charmed out of their small clothes with ease in Thalonia.

"They can be, but war is always a threat there, and Taux is a free city and haunted," Erik replied.

"Yes, the Minions of the Jackal lurk among those lands…" she broke off.

Erik nodded glancing at Tavalori as the young man wove through the tall swamp grass ahead.

"Minions of a dark god are a constant threat, but the last war was said to be the end of the Jackal's games of conquest," Erik said.

Anais rode in silence a moment before she spoke again. "Isn't that also what was said after the Battle of Thunder Fields and the dawning of the Fifth Age?"

She knows her history… I'll credit her instructors that much…

"True, the Jackal has a way of finding portals back into this realm," Erik answered.

"You speak of him without much regard," she said.

Erik frowned and then gave a soft laugh. "I worship the Lady of Felines, and like me she finds the reins of responsibility and the Lord of Jackals to be a complete bore."

Raziel suddenly brought his steed up to block the two of them, the thick-set bard staring Erik down as he did so.

"Perhaps you should see if the young woodsman needs any guidance since you seem to know so much about the realm and the god's who play in it," Raziel said.

Erik's hand itched to grab the hilt of his blade, but instead he offered a quick bow before moving forward to catch Tavalori further up the twisting dirt road.

Behind him a whispered yet heated exchange took place between Anais and her companion, but he was too far out of earshot to hear it.

Stay close Malcolm, I'll want a report on what they say before my first night watch…

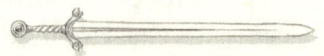

The road had twisted and fallen away to nothing more times than Erik could remember, but on each occasion Tavalori kept them on course and away from danger. As a company they moved well, Tavalori scouting the trail, Erik leading the riders, and Braxus and Malcolm bringing up the rear with the pony-bound Ash.

The Eldaryn talked constantly as they moved along fens, preaching the will of Bandylegs and the blessings of that trickster god. His constant proselytizing was being broken only by bellowed curses from Braxus and calming words from Malcolm.

Raziel didn't say a word after the fight with Anais, but Erik watched him as he kept a tight hold of the reins of the pair's horses.

"Tower," Tavalori called from further up the trail.

Raziel and Erik both stopped short as Tavalori moved back to them, his strung bow in hand.

"It's an old sea tower," the young man said.

"It must be one of old King Froust NyWinter's towers built when he defended the west of Aflyr from Corsairs in the Age of Dragons," Anais interjected.

"Nice piece of history." snapped Raziel sarcastically, adding "But what does that mean to us?"

Tavalori leaned on his bow and shot a look back at the tower which was just visible in the distance.

"We've passed a dozen other tower ruins along our journey, but this is the first one that's still intact. Also, there are signs of Delvers along the eastern path of the tower and the main door has been smashed off its hinges," he answered.

Drawing his blade from its sheath, Erik called back to Braxus and Malcolm, "Delvers!"

Raziel nearly choked, asking, "What in the name of the gods do you think you are doing?"

"Investigating," Erik replied.

Tavalori nocked an arrow and the other two mercenaries moved forward with blades in hand.

"You can't be serious? We should go around. There is no reason..." Raziel argued before being cut short as Anais drew a thin blade from its resting place in her saddle gear.

Erik assessed the blade before recognizing the kingfisher of Lystbrook etched across the hand-guard.

"We're going as well, Raziel," she said.

Raziel cursed under his breath but drew his own blade from his saddle-bags. He was still shaking his head when he said, "Miss Atara, this is crazy."

"If Masters Erik and Tavalori think it worth having a look then so do I," she replied.

Erik turned toward the tower, "You heard the lady."

"I'll stay with the horses," Ash said.

The riders came to ground and Ash muttered prayers for luck as he took the reins and fell back to wait among the tall grass.

Boots sloshed across the mucky fen before scraping against stone as they crossed a low perimeter wall and then made their way up the gentle grass-covered slope to what remained of a small terrace. The dark stone was mottled with a deep yellow mold, the grass high and no discernible trail leading up to the shattered door.

If someone lives here, they've forgotten long ago how to maintain the dwelling... Erik thought.

Tavalori was first to the tower. Moving alongside the damaged door, he pressed his back to the stone and nodded for the rest of them to advance. Malcolm and Braxus worked their way closer, and Erik hung back with Raziel and Anais in a high crop of cattails.

Tavalori ducked low, his head peeking inside before he pulled back his bowstring and let loose a shaft.

His string sang and a low grunt was followed by the clanking of armor. Tavalori fell back as a massive Delver burst through the door. The creature was low slung, no more than five feet with broad shoulders and skin the color of bedrock. The overwhelming scent of newly tilled earth oozed from its black iron plates, and it was armored from sloped brow to wide foot.

It raised a great axe toward the woodsman but Malcolm was on it, the mercenary's broadsword catching the creature in the chain links at the armpit and drawing an angry grunt. Braxus came in from the far side, his own sword used like a spear as he drove it point-first into a gap in the creature's leg armor. The Delver tipped sideways, his axe slipping from his fingers as he fell to the ground. Blades rose and fell on him, Braxus and Malcolm finishing the fight as Tavalori covered the entrance with another nocked arrow.

Mounting the terrace, Erik advanced and whispered, "Delver's this deep into the north?"

Malcolm shook his head, "Nehru is the bottleneck… Delvers shouldn't have been able to come past the fortress in number, but a small band might slip through the smaller trails."

Nodding, Erik raised his blade and moved inside. The air was over-whelmed with an earthy odor, but a hint of pungently salty sea essence was noticeable as well. His eyes adjusted quickly to the dim chamber, the bottom level was part kitchen and part sleeping area with a few scattered books that had been ripped and thrown on the floor.

From above there were heavy voices and the sound of boots pounding the wooden planks ten feet over his head. Another Delver lay dead near the near the base of the wooden stairs, an arrow sticking out of its bloody faceplate.

"Looks like you'll get a chance to dance today Fury…" Erik whispered to his blade.

The weapon shone dimly in the gloom of the interior, dark-etched runes drawing in light along its broadest point near the silvered hilt.

Boots started down the stairs and Erik quickly slipped beneath the wooden steps pressing his back against the curved stone wall. The creature was halfway down the steps when another arrow sang across the chamber, this one toppled the armored enemy off the stairs and sent him thudding to the floor near Erik's feet.

The Delver clutched in vain at the projectile jutting from its throat, but Erik ended its suffering with a quick downward strike that nearly severed its neck. The earthy odor of the dead Delver at his feet gagged him, but he went back to his hiding place as agitated shouts sounded from above.

At the door, Malcolm leaned in and hissed, "How many?"

Erik shrugged and raised four fingers. Above, more boots began moving down the stair. Another arrow whistled in, this one only causing a curse. Erik brought *Fury* forward, readying himself as the first set of heavy boots appeared in the openings between each step.

He stabbed the back of the Delver's calf just above the rim of its boots, the creature tumbling forward as the blow threw him off-balance. Two other Delvers leapt off the stairs and crashed to the stone floor like iron titans, shields ready and scimitars forward.

"Flank!" Erik yelled.

The first Delver turned and brought the full weight of his ire to bear against the defense of Erik's *Fury*, the broadsword sparking with the im-

pact. Unable to fall back, Erik adjusted his weapon to a two-handed grip and braced for another blow.

Behind him Braxus and Malcolm clashed with the other Delver who'd jumped down the stair, and yet a fifth was half down the short span barking unintelligible orders at the rest. Erik saw a flash of movement, Anais racing to the foot of the stair with her rapier in hand.

"No!" he called.

The stair-bound Delver knocked the girl's weapon from her hand with a sweeping stroke of his great-axe, and Anais fell back into Raziel who brought his sword around to ward off a second blow.

Erik's Delver struck at him a third time, this blow biting stone near his shoulder, and he used the weight of the enemy's attack to swing *Fury* at its chest. The Delver caught the sword with his shield and the stink of earth began to saturate the closed air of the room.

The Delver spat some insult and swung again but his blade went high and lodged into the wood of the stair just above Erik's head. Striking up, Erik severed the hand holding the scimitar. Blood sprayed the wall as his enemy fell back and Erik pressed his advantage with two quick strokes to the creature's heavy helm. Either stunned or dead, the Delver toppled forward and moved no more.

Quickly, Erik moved to aid Raziel, whose defenses were clearly waning. With the enemy distracted, Erik raised his inverted sword high in a two handed grip and brought it plunging down. Point first, the blade sunk into the Delver at the base of his neck and didn't stop until it could go no further. The axe fell from limp hands as the Delver slumped forward and crashed at the feet of Raziel.

"One more to go," Erik said.

Behind him Malcolm and Braxus had their Delver backed into a wall, the thing's shield dented and the stones around it were cracked from elemental magic. Earth-stink permeated the area, and Erik's lungs were thick with it as he struggled to breathe. The two mercenary's blades hammered away at the creature, but the elemental defense pushed back their blows.

"He's calling the earth, stay back," Erik warned.

Raziel kept Anais behind him and Erik stepped into the combat, *Fury* raised, as Malcolm hammered away at the Delver's defense. A part of the wall cracked and loose stones tumbled to the ground, whatever magic the Delver was using was draining strength from the surrounding stone to bolster his defense.

Braxus matched Malcolm's attacks, and the stone continued to crumble.

He'll take us all with him if he can… Erik thought.

Erik saw an opening and went low bringing *Fury* against the stone-hard shin guards of the Delver's armor. They sparked and half-turned his strike but the magic of his own blade resisted the elemental thickening enough to snap the bone beneath.

The Delver fell, Braxus and Malcolm at last finding purchase for their blades, again and again, until the thing lay still.

"Gods of fire, that one was tough," Braxus said.

"We're lucky the rest of them weren't so elementally attuned or this would have gone very differently," Erik said.

Raziel helped Anais to her feet, and Tavalori entered the chamber with an arrow still pulled against his bowstring. Erik kicked a corpse and moved about the room searching as his boots scraped the rugs aside before revealing an iron ring set in the stone floor. Looking back, he saw Braxus tying a bandage on his left arm and Malcolm ascending the stair to the second level.

I guess I'll just have a little look…

He knelt, his fingers wrapping around the ring and giving it a pull. Instead of flagstone as he had surmised, the trap door was slate over wood and his yank lifted the door much farther than he would have liked.

Light flashed from the darkness below and a blast of amber energy shot forth and blew a hole in the ceiling above. Erik slammed the trap door back down with a resounding thud.

"You ok?" Tavalori asked.

Erik checked himself with a quick pat down but nodded, "Yes… but obviously something's down there."

Tavalori took a step closer just as Malcolm looked down through the still smoking hole in the ceiling.

Erik looked up at the mercenary above, asking, "Anything?"

"A woman's body is up here, and some drug cookery, but from the look of her the Delvers didn't give her much time before they fell on her with blades aplenty," Malcolm answered.

The smell of salt-water was seeping up from beneath the floor. Erik nodded up at Malcolm, saying, "That explains a lot, get down here will yah?"

Malcolm descended and Tavalori held his bow on the trap door.

"What's down there?" Malcolm asked.

"Maybe an apprentice," Erik answered.

Malcolm raised an eyebrow.

"A water-witch, that's bad luck. I say we leave her down there," Braxus spat.

Erik waved the mercenary to silence and then leaned a bit toward the door, "I know you can hear me. We're not your enemy. The Delvers are dead."

The party watched the portal. After almost a minute the slate lifted a couple of inches.

"Where's my Mistress?" The voice of a young woman asked from within.

Erik looked at Malcolm who only shrugged, "If you mean the woman upstairs, I'm afraid she's with her gods."

The door stayed in position for a minute before the girl below spoke again.

"What is your name?" she asked.

"Erik," he replied.

Anais stepped forward slapping Raziel's warding hand away. "And I'm Anais Atara. You're safe, I give you my word."

The door opened further and a lean-faced figure framed with dark hair appeared. She looked no more than twenty winters, her eyes a deep green and the plated folds of her hair were pulled back with silver combs.

The young woman tipped her head to Anais, "M'lady?"

Anais smiled, "I'm no court lady, just a simple singer."

The girl looked around at the party, her pale skin touched with the slightest hint of blue around her jaw and over her eyes.

"Do you have a name?" Anais asked.

The girl blinked, color rushing to her cheeks and the tang of salt once again filling the room, "I apologize... my name is Telluria, Telluria Mistral, apprentice to Magi Xandra of the Tristra Tower."

Braxus grunted, "At least she's is only a petty witch."

Telluria's eyes grew wide, but Erik stepped between her and Braxus, "It's just the way he talks, and he's never been around a true water-born before."

"You're all human?" she asked.

"Fire spirits all," Erik replied.

She nodded. Her expression remained vacant but Anais reached forward and offered the woman her hand, "It's fine, we're not as bad as you've probably heard."

Telluria reached out and touched Anais's hand, the two exchanging a moment of knowledge as their elemental spirits contacted.

"The sun is on the fall," Tavalori interrupted. "And there were only six Delvers here, which is half a standard raiding band."

"Right," Erik said. He looked at Telluria, "Have you anything you need from this place?"

"No, everything one of my race needs comes from within," she answered.

Braxus rolled his eyes and muttered, "Looks like her mistress needed a bit more than what she carried." Malcolm grabbed Braxus and started shoving him toward the door.

Erik nodded, "Fine, then let's be away before more trouble shows up that we're unequipped to deal with."

Erik left Telluria in Anais's care as he cleaned *Fury* and returned the blade to its sheath on the way to the door. Outside, Ash was holding a conversation with the horses as he walked up the ruined path toward the door.

"Our company grows," the woodsman said.

"In both size and stature," Erik replied, "if you believe in the power of the Order of Towers." He looked back, "Still, this girl isn't much like any Wizard I've ever seen."

Tavalori looked back at Raziel, whispering, "Looks can be deceiving."

"Yeah, they're certainly not common minstrels," Erik said.

"Noble?" Tavalori asked.

"Maybe, but at this point I wouldn't stake my blade on it," Erik answered.

"Why would they masquerade?" Tavalori asked.

Erik shrugged, "What else is there for a young prince or princess to do but play at being a common hero?"

"Only a fool would give up a life like that," Tavalori said.

Erik nodded, a slight smile on his face.

A fool or someone hiding from something worse than the bonds of honor that tie all nobility...

CHAPTER FOUR

SAFFRON

I'm pretty… no really, I'm pretty right? I can almost see you lurking like a shade behind my shoulder as I stare into this mirror.

No answer?

Gods… why do I even try? I'm probably going insane. The king says my father was a simple fisherman who drowned himself rather than take care of his only daughter alone. That sounds pretty crazy right, like it's in my blood…

Now I'm talking to spooks, feeling eyes on me as I stand here half-dressed without a purpose in life other than find a suitable husband.

I was supposed to be something special, something different. I protected the princess, I was her shield for five years as well as her handmaiden and now I'm reduced to nothing. She's gone and I'm here, an interloper in a court of true ladies and noble sires.

Yet there you hover, like a shimmer of the light on the sea stones in August. Isn't there something you can tell me? Am I to be done, at eighteen winters, resigning myself to servitude and babies until one steals the last life from me. That's no swordsman's death, and yet I'm a shield-maiden, so perhaps a different end comes for us.

I cannot say and you will not either, so an end to it then. Back to life, whatever life that may be…

Saffron turned once more, her reflection in the spotted silver dressing mirror drawing a curl to her thin lip as her hands moved to her breasts.

"I might as well be a man," she whispered, her palms finding only the slight curve in her dressing gown.

She was skinny but strong. Her days were spent in the castle yard with the king's squires playing at swords which kept her lithe and whip like.

"Miserable..." she stated.

Stalking to her dresser she withdrew a pair of breeches, a thick doublet, and a cloak, tossing each onto her bed. Slipping off her nightdress, she put on the comfortable clothing and finished the outfit with a pair of high, metal-heeled leather boots.

Her slender fingers applied combs to her hair, dark like Aligo chocolate, before turning to her bedpost for her blade. She sighed, picked up the sword and left the room. The sound of metal striking stone echoed down the passage as she made her way to the lady's foyer.

It was a circular chamber with a high, domed ceiling. Mermaids and other fanciful sea-creatures were painted in frescos above each of the eight openings. None of the archways held doors save the largest one, which held a pair of heavy wood and bronze doubles that could be bolted from the other side.

"Saffron!" Jane called from another room, "Igrayn is gone, come be with us as there's no need for your sword this day!"

More voices echoed the request made by Jane, the youngest of the ladies in waiting and Saffron turned to look in the direction of their voices. Through the arched opening that led to Verin's room, she could see all seven of the ladies in waiting, perched amid a sea of violet and aquamarine colored cushions. Verin the subtle, eldest of the ladies, at twenty-two winters, lay upon a divan of creamy silk, a long-haired cat in her lap.

"I'm well aware of Igrayn's departure from these halls," Saffron replied.

"Then don't carry yourself about like a squire and join us. The time of defense is no more, and we must prepare for the coming wedding of our lady," Rosund said.

Rosund was blond and petite, with breasts like swollen melons, a point that often made men both young and old act stupidly in her presence.

"The wedding is not for another ten months, and I've better things to do than gossip about the grey king of Aflyr," Saffron said.

"She's being a bore as usual," Prish said.

Saffron turned to eye the water-born Corsair's daughter, her face lean and her hair slicked back, dark like the wet hide of a seal.

"Hold your tongue, fishmonger, or I'll take it out," Saffron hissed.

Prish stood, but Verin held her with a look and Avril, a tall ginger-haired and frosty daughter of a Tundarian ivory merchant pulled Prish away from the door.

"What trouble have we caused you to act thus?" Verin asked.

Saffron's lips tightened, "I hold our lady's safety and happiness in the highest regard, and yet you seem to find pleasure in auctioning her off to the highest bidder as though it's a just and joyous occasion," she said.

Verin's face was pale and mirthless with eyes dark and yet smoldering like the embers of a dying fire.

"We cannot change our fate, Lady Saffron, and throwing ourselves against such debts of nobility will only cause pain. My sisters and I wish to bring as much joy to a troublesome mandate as we are able, and yet you would what… march against another nation with a single blade to save our lady from their just and righteous king? And who is to say that she will not grow accustomed to her new life, or even to love her new husband?"

Saffron let her fingers brush against the hilt of her sword and Lady Jane sucked in a tiny breath but Verin continue to glare.

The two young women stared at each other a long moment before Saffron turned on her heel and stormed out, calling over her shoulder as she went, "I've yet to meet a god or goddess, and so I say fate be damned. There are those that say that Humans and Corsairs control our own destiny and so I will take action."

The ladies murmured behind her, but she kept walking, the resounding echoes of her boot heels signaling her passing until she hit the carpeted runners of the Queen's descent.

Fools… they send Igrayn away and trust her keeping to a Citadel Knight while a man twice her age waits for her return like a slavering hound across the border? For all my love of the Queen, it was foolish and dangerous to trust that Igrayn would be safe with a single bodyguard at the house of her aged great aunt. Knowing my princess as I do, she wouldn't dwell in that coastal keep long before she fled on some ridiculous dream of truly living.

Quickening her pace she passed the queen's solar where floor to ceiling windows opened toward the sea and the call of gulls drifted through silken drapes. The hall then gave way to a terraced patio surrounded by open lawns and russet gardens.' Winter had muted all the splendor and colorful fanfare of the summer greenery.

This whole mess stinks of something foul. King Ergoroth, as much as he ignores his daughter, should have intervened to keep her here. He risks everything if something happens to her and the impending alliance with Alfyr is broken... its madness, and that entire family is embroiled in it.

From beyond the walls triangle-sailed fishing boats plied the waters and smaller craft lay in anchor amid the kelp fields as divers searched out abalone and clams.

Saffron brushed a peacock from her path, the large male twitching his tail feathers as he leapt onto a pillared stone wall.

"Save your threats, my beauty, like all men you're more pomp than action," she whispered.

Further down the path she went, passing from the regality of the Queen's Bastion through a gateway and into the King's Stead. A practice yard lay adjacent to the stables and was surrounded by thick and straight-cut walls where knightly banners and armed men strode in small companies of polished helms and pointed lances.'

"Lady Saffron," a man called.

She turned to see Sir Talron limping toward her, one of the few men in the King's court she cared to smile upon. He bowed his square face to kiss her hand.

She consented, "M'Lord."

"What brings you to the Stead this day?" he asked.

"I'm in need of a hard ride."

"I am always ready to oblige you lady Saffron," he replied with a sly look.

"You know what I mean Sir Talron," she replied, a smile twitching the corner of her lips.

"Aye, I do. But if you'll insist on things your way, then take Highstorm, that mare is as spirited as you and she's in need of a good running!"

"Thank you!" she called back. She held up a hand in farewell as she turned and continued on her way, but she could feel the man's gaze follow her all the way to the stable door.

If you were not a king's man I'd give you more time, but today leaves me little patience for anyone from these bartered and sold walls...

Saffron tucked her scabbard beneath the saddlebag and placed the open-faced helm on the pommel of the saddle. The young grooms watched her but said nothing, their attention only on the way she readied her mare for a journey.

With a gloved hand she massaged the horse's white snout and whispered words of kindness in her pointed ears.

"Lady Saffron," a man's voice interrupted her communion.

She didn't turn, instead moving back to the saddle and rechecking the straps.

The man was nearer in the second speaking, "Saffy, didn't you hear me?"

Turning, she gave a slight nod, "Prince Wilam…"

"Going somewhere?" he asked.

"I thought to take a ride down to the sea and give Sir Talron's horse some salt on her legs."

He reached up and tried to stroke the horse's face but it pulled away.

"With a blade and helm?" he asked.

"Is there a problem?"

He was as handsome as his sister Igrayn was fair but his eyes held the same hollow fire as his father, amber and wild.

He reached up to touch her face, "Saffy…"

She pushed his hand aside, saying, "Saffron."

His eyes flashed and the sea stormed in her veins as Wilam's heat bloomed between them.

"Just because you're my sister's chosen protector and a self-proclaimed 'lord' of the squires, don't presume to correct me in such a fashion. I'm still your crown prince."

She forced a smile and bowed her head slightly, though never lowering her eyes from his. His heat brought bile to her throat, the Corsair blood in her veins was of the water and directly opposed to his short-lived and consuming fire-spark.

"Better," he said inclining his head.

He smiled and let his eye roam over the soft skin of her pale neck.

"Is there a reason you always run away from me?"

Her stomach did flips but she couldn't stop herself from saying, "Just because you have found some easy success seducing your sister's handmaidens does not mean that all women find you irresistible! Go bother Verin, Prish, or Catyrin if you need someone to warm your bed."

He leaned in toward her, running the tip of his finger down the collar of her shirt, his face almost touching hers and whispered, "I won them with my charms, but with you perhaps I should claim my right of dominion as crown prince..."

Quick as a viper, she tipped her face down and smashed the top of her head up into his face. The pair of groomsmen sucked breath between their teeth as the prince jerked back clutching his nose, blood flowing through his fingers. His expression, moments earlier so smug, was now seething with anger.

Heat bloomed like a summer day and Wilam lunged at her. She ducked away and instead he struck the hindquarters of the horse. The beast kicked back, its hoof catching the prince in the midsection, dropping him in a cursing and gasping heap at her feet.

Grooms shouted and raced to the fallen prince, but Saffron mounted her horse and wheeled it around until she again faced Wilam.

For a moment their eyes met, his filled with murder and hers with disgust. Breaking the wordless exchange she put the heels of her boots into the horse's sides and galloped from the stable in a great rush.

Mercenaries and castle regulars broke from her path like water before the prow of a ship, her mount bursting from the main gate and racing down the twisting cobbled streets of Sastrine. Her mare's stride was pitched as though the demons of the Burning City were at her back and she hung low against the saddle as wind drew tears from her eyes.

She made it to the woods a quarter mile from the capital city before the first horns blew from the battlements of the castle. With a final look back, she said a prayer to the Sea Mistress for deliverance before she plunged into the headlands of the Wintertide.

Igrayn... my princess...I'm sorry but the madness has taken them all and I pray it has not gone with you as well.

Her horse beat a path into the woods, branches catching and cutting her face and clothing but she stayed hard on the mare. The winter air colored her cheeks and her hands ached in knotted balls against the reins but she continued on, splashing through cold streams and purple brambles. The day drew down in long shadows before she let up and slowed her course, her mount covered in lather and a froth of white spit clung around its mouth.

Foolish girl... she cursed herself.

Jerking the reins stiffly she brought the horse to a sudden stop. The forest sat silent as she leapt from the beast's back and fell to her knees, the contents of her stomach emptying onto the leaf-covered ground.

She retched again, her mind spinning at the images of the prince on his back and the hatred in his eyes dashed against her sanity like waves on the breakwater.

Igrayn, what have I done?

Several minutes passed as her breathing deepened, fingers digging into the leaves beneath her.

If I were an odd pariah before, I'm a murderous assassin now... Igrayn, I can't go back, not without you to protect me and how foolish is that since I've always been the one to shield you?

She got her footing and returned to Highstorm. Whispering soft words, she soothed the mare as best she could before again gaining the saddle. She gave a gentle nudge from her heels and the horse limped forward. The game trail led deeper into the hills of the southern Wintertide, the cold afternoon light doing little to warm her spirits.

Wilam won't come in here, not even with hate driving him on... I'll use the forest, keeping under its venerable boughs until I reach the far side and the Aflyrian border. There, I'll set things right when I find you Igrayn...

CHAPTER FIVE

ERIK

*Y*eah, *I know what you're wondering, why didn't I make a move on Telluria? Well, if you were here you'd know straight away. She's a Wizard, and Wizards mean high water, the opposition element to all things human. Sure, we humans might be considered low fire but that doesn't mean we have to like a high water, which is to say I might throw in with a low water Corsair, but high water is like touching dead fish.*

Besides, I've still got Anais to deal with, and it seems with each passing hour she grows more dreamy-eyed about Tavalori. I don't get it, as the guy is nothing to look at, but I guess he's closer her age and does have an honorable innocence about him, although I don't trust his spark... yes, definitely something strange there...

Anyway, if you're back that means something important must be on the horizon so I'll keep Fury close at hand...

The ladies talked as the coast opened up around them, scattered with farms and trade roads. All paths now lead toward the distant walls and towers of the city of Mahe some fifty leagues to their north, but this was still rough country and from the look, mostly deserted as well.

Erik, taking up a position just to the rear of Anais's mare, listened to their conversation as small birds played a game of tag among the swamp grass.

"His hands were so strong," Anais was saying.

She cast a look ahead to where Tavalori scouted the road. Raziel was forward of the pair, talking with Malcolm, the man making motions like he was fighting something as the mercenary nodded.

"It must be his use of the bow. Not only would that give him powerful hands but also strong arms," Telluria replied.

"I wonder if he has a woman somewhere, some stout bride in a cabin of thick wood," Anais mused.

Telluria shrugged, "If he does, he makes no mention of her around the fire."

Anais looked sharply at the apprentice Wizard, "Do tell?"

"Last night as I sharpened the knives after dinner I overheard Erik and Tavalori talking about their homes. Although Erik said very little other than he'd traveled so long he barely remembered his home, Tavalori stated that he'd left his lonely house very recently to see the world and find adventure outside the realm of the forest."

Anais bit her lip, "Adventure…"

Telluria nodded, "Perhaps you should sing him a love song and then draw him away into a field before we reach the city, or better yet you could slink away to a private room when we acquire one at a fine Mahe Inn."

The songstress let her gaze travel from Tavalori to Raziel, "I doubt that would be possible…"

Telluria followed her eyes until she too was looking on the hulking minstrel.

"What hold has he over you?"

Anais waited a moment before shaking her head, "He sees himself as my protector, and although I will do as I please, he may still try to stop me."

"Then you must find a way to convince him otherwise," Telluria said.

Anais frowned, "What will happen is in the hands of the fates, but that doesn't mean we have to only discuss me and my wants."

"Meaning?" Telluria asked.

"Meaning, what of Erik?"

Telluria's pale skin blushed deep violet along her chin and the arch of her ears. "What are you talking about?"

Anais looked around, and Erik ducked behind her horse, the beast's dung-ridden tale striking him in the face. He stifled a gag and held himself close until she turned back around.

"I'm sure I'm not the only one who's let her thoughts wander to the handsome men of our company. Erik has a look about him, tall, sandy-haired, and a face that would keep many a lady's attention for years on end."

Telluria shook her head, "No... I couldn't dream of such a thing, I'm a Wizard after all."

"Water and Fire might not make children, but that difficulty might be more of a blessing if you value your freedom."

Erik raised a brow... *now those are words of a free spirit I hadn't expected...*

"I'm of the Order, and we're not allowed such pleasures while we still wear the linen garb of an apprentice."

Anais shook her head, "Is there no way? How would they even know?"

Telluria sighed, "Like you I am protected, but my defender has a thousand eyes and the magic of the ages, or so my mistress told me on various occasions. There are sure to be Order Wizards in Mahe, and if I come to them touched by the hand of another element they will have ways of knowing. I cannot afford to be thrown out, as my only family has been the teachers of the Order. They've known me since I was born in the Rat Piers of ChanderNagor."

"Rat Piers? I thought they burned down a century ago... How old are you?" Anais asked.

"One hundred and twenty-nine," Telluria whispered.

There was a long moment of silence before Anais said, "Then water is eternal?"

"No, only air is forever, but those of the high water are still very slow to age."

They road on a few minutes in silence before Anais spoke again, "I've never been to ChanderNagor but I hear it's a beautiful place."

"It's a wondrous city, and the Palace Hill is circled by white walls and colorful gardens, although only the very rich may enter them," Telluria said.

"I'm certain I will see it soon enough..." Anais said.

"Is something wrong?"

"No, I simply draw myself too far into the future. A trip to Chander-Nagor is not in my cards for the morrow, and so the honor of my company belongs to Mahe and the splendors of the western coast, at least for now," Anais answered.

Ahead Tavalori called for a halt, their path now curving around a low hill that was capped by another crumbled tower and stone wall. To the west, the sun hung low in the sky above the fens and the smell of the sea drifted on the evening breeze.

"Time for a rest, Anais," Raziel said.

Ash spoke up right behind Erik making him jump, "And a better time couldn't have been wished for as my friend Braxus and I were about to share a drink from my wineskin in toast to great Bran Bandylegs."

The ladies turned to look first at Ash and then Erik, both of their eyes lingering on him.

"Very well, I think we should heed the suggestion of these gentlemen and take a break," Anais said.

Sliding her legs over the polished leather surface of the saddle, she slipped toward the ground. Before her boots touched the earth, Tavalori caught her by the waist and lowered her slowly down.

Raziel had taken the reins of the horse while she dismounted, and his displeasure at the woodsman's action was clear by the look in his eyes and the heat that bloomed from his shoulders, but he said nothing.

Tavalori and Anais locked eyes for a fleeting moment before he released her. Anais flushed and looked down while Tavalori turned away to help grab equipment from the saddlebags of the two horses.

Telluria jumped down as well, her hand being caught by Malcolm who'd suddenly appeared beside her horse.

"One more night and Mahe will be ours," Malcolm said.

She nodded and drew back her hand. Erik watched the exchange and then marched with the others up the hill toward the ruined tower, as crickets sang among the scattered stones.

Dead grass waved in the breeze as Erik watched Malcolm pick mud from the rim of his boot with a stick. The rest of the small party stretched their legs among the stones, the sun's orange afterglow mixing with the violet of the early evening clouds.

"I've never met a true member of the Order of Towers," Ash said.

Telluria looked down at the Eldaryn and smiled.

"And you still have not, as I'm only an apprentice and not yet initiated into the Order," she replied.

Ash scratched his chin, "What does it mean to be initiated?"

Telluria stared out over the marshes in the direction of the distant sea. Fog was rolling in like a grey blanket in the dying light.

"Once you've completed your apprenticeship under the tutelage of an Order member, you're accepted in one of three houses, each dedicated to a different school of thought concerning magic and its use," she replied.

"And yet I use magic and have never been honored with a request to join the Order," Ash said.

"Your magic is faith derived, the gift of your god," Raziel broke in.

Telluria nodded, adding, "My magic is a force beyond my elemental realm, a well of power that drifts beyond nature and between the gods… the Afterglow Sea."

Ash stared at her but no words were forthcoming.

Finally, she said, "Let me explain…"

Ash brightened and even Erik and Malcolm turned their attention to her.

"Let me first address the gods," Telluria began, "The greater powers beyond this plane are creatures who grant gifts to their worshippers when the link is strong enough to allow for such things."

"Meaning priests." Malcolm said.

"Unless she means anyone with extreme faith," Braxus offered.

"Yes and no. You see faith is a powerful tool, and it's said a god will provide gifts of protection, balance, and equity to any worshipper that has the faith to pull such power across the astral planes," Telluria corrected.

"I've never had any gods bestow magic gifts on me when I asked for it," Braxus complained as he ran a whetstone down the blade of his sword.

Malcolm cut in, "Braxus, when have you ever even thought about a god?"

"I think about them sometimes," he replied, "usually when I am about to get beaten to a bloody pulp!"

Malcolm and Braxus snorted with laughter.

Ash shushed the mercenaries, "She said if your faith was *strong* enough."

Braxus grunted and went back to his sharpening as Malcolm rolled his eyes.

Telluria went on, "Braxus is correct in theory; although I've never seen such a thing in practice either."

"And what of the Druids?" Erik asked.

Telluria paused a moment before she addressed Erik's question. "All Druids worship a god called the Oak Father, but he is only an additive to their true power. They draw their magic from beyond the ethereal rivers, the bulk of their magic channeled out of the elemental planes of fire, air, earth, and water."

"Each race comes from a single elemental force most commonly called a spark, even for those of water. You all know how it is… Humans are low fire, Wizards high water, Delvers are low earth, and Aspara high air, but a Druid is different. Druids are amalgamations. They are able to crossbreed, creating offspring that share heritage in two elements. The Oak Father increases their power like any god, but their faith in him doesn't dictate their level of magic. Only their true understanding of elemental channeling determines that."

"That still hasn't explained your magic," Ash said.

Telluria shook her head, her long brown hair falling down into her face before she reflexively tucked it back behind her ear. When she drew her fingers away, they bore the sheen of water.

"No, Master Ash, it has not," she began. "The magic of the Order, and even the Tome Mages, is something entirely different. Our magic is drawn from the *Afterglow*, a reservoir of raw power like nothing else in the universe. That power is a chaotic maelstrom of force that's located far beyond the border of the Elemental Plane of Water. For that reason, those creatures bound to water as their element can better utilize its power than any other race.

"The Order instructs water-born in the use of such power, in shaping it like an artist works a canvas, giving Wizards the ability to do incredible things with their intrinsic abilities. This process is dangerous, however, and the Wizards' lives depend on their ability to control the magic so that it does not overwhelm them," she finished.

Ash shook his head, "So your magic can kill you?"

Raziel, rummaging through his pack, said, "If you consider the *Afterglow* to be an ocean, and this world we live in the dam that holds it back from crushing us all, then the Wizards are the release gates that can let some of the water flow out into our world safely."

All eyes turned to the large man, and Telluria offered a slight smile before she broke the stares, saying, "Yes, Raziel is exactly right, but there is a little more involved. A Wizard actually becomes a storage vessel for that power, and the stronger they are, the more energy they can hold and then use at their disposal."

Raziel jumped back in again, "The only trouble is that some Wizards try to draw directly from the *Afterglow* instead of leeching power off and storing it correctly. When this happens, the Wizard's body pays the price for channeling raw energy beyond what his corporal existence can handle."

He finally looked up, the party watching him. There was a moment of pause, his hand flexing as his dark eyes grew wide, and he realized that he had said too much. Anais broke the tense silence following his revelation, asking, "Can a Wizard be killed by this channeling?"

Telluria turned from Raziel to the young songstress, "Yes, and many more are withered, aged, or brain damaged by such a foolish exchange."

"But why would they do such a thing?" Ash asked.

Telluria shook her head, "Power is an addictive force, and I would think many of those who are so reckless can't help the surge of greatness they experience by wielding magic far above their abilities."

"Or perhaps it's about love," Erik said.

The entire group turned to him and he grinned, "Or hate, or dire need. Look, if a beast was attacking you, and your own reserves were depleted, what choice would you have other than drawing on the raw power?"

Telluria's eyes glowed emerald in the firelight, the smell of salty brine heavy about the camp.

"True again, Master Erik," she stated.

Erik smiled at her, "I'm no master."

She nodded and looked away. Night was on the rise and the conversation died as the fire smoked among the ruin-stones. Ash tried to rekindle the conversation several times but no one showed interest, the day's march drawing cloaks around shoulders and heads to blankets.

Erik watched each of his companions fall into their own thoughts, except for Anais who continued whispering to Tavalori until Raziel broke them apart.

The girl wants him, and I want her, but my act of nonchalance hasn't worked and she's slipping away…she must be one of those that wants to be chased.

He rolled into his cloak, the night turning cold as the Ghost Moon rose into the sky. All around he felt the penetrating influence of water and it turned his stomach.

Once we get to Mahe, I've got to find a way to get some time alone with Anais. Maybe Braxus and Malcolm can get Raziel overly drunk and keep him out of my way… but Tavalori? How am I to get rid of him?

CHAPTER SIX

RELAN

Y*ou are here but you are not the Oak Father... there is little nature in you, only the smattering that comes rising from the earth and
returning to it at the end of days.*

*What does that mean then, that you're something beyond a god or
something less? Whatever the answer, I feel you walking with me, beyond me, around me as I take this course beneath the ancient stands
of oak, pine, ash, and silver tower.*

*Have you come seeking my prey as well? Are you some magic
agent of the boy's mother, some succubus or hound demon slinking in
my path only to leap forth at an opportune time?*

I doubt this as well, for no benevolence is within you...

*Follow then but keep patient, for my days among the wood are
long, tedious, and without companionship or pleasant conversation.
This is the way of the druid, and I walk it alone as all those of my
coven have since the Age of Mists...*

The hills were still touched with frost and the remaining brown and
gold leaves in the thickets shone white in the morning light. A stand of pin
oaks held their leaves defiantly against the late fall temperatures, and winds
buffeted by the surrounding hills whistled down into a grotto where Relan
was beginning to awake from his slumber.

He stretched, the staff in his hand steaming in the cold morning air.

"Keep your fires stoked, old friend, the journey is still long and the days grow colder," Relan said.

The staff hummed, the trio of twisting fire-birds atop the shaft catching the morning light.

"My life is a lonely one, but you somehow keep me company... even if you never reply to my ramblings," he said.

Giving a final long stretch, he moved from the shelter of the pines to the more skeletal forest around.

"*Phoenix*, tell me my path is true," he said.

The end of the staff began to glow and within it a tendril of white-fire shot away through the trees to the west. A horn blew in the distance and howls drifted on the breeze.

I hear the Lowl hunting to the east, but the Well of Ages is close... no more than an hour and I'll have some answers to my questions concerning the boy and his venture into the lands of humanity...

His feet crunched old leaves, and the Lowl's calls kept driving him on as most of the forest world still slept in burrow and nest against the chill of early winter. He moved among timbers on the valley floor, his staff showing the way as here and there tall druid stones rose up and told voiceless tales of the proximity to his current destination.

The entire area was ancient and alive, each tree towering up over him like a sentinel guarding against intrusion. Druid stones were everywhere, crooked and pocked, the work of his long-forgotten brethren still holding court among the bowers of the venerable Wintertide. Each dark block was carved by hand and covered in runes, now worn down by the passing of ages. Brown lichen snaked up from the ground and wrapped around the stones like dead fingers.

He waded through a sea of monoliths, the sacred well tucked inside a final full ring the breadth of a Human city square. The circular wall of the tranquil well was made of dark stone, the watery surface inside like glass, reflecting the blue and white sky above it with perfect clarity.

Kneeling down beside the well, he laid his staff on the ground and moved the sleeves of his tunic up past his elbows.

"Oak Father, I call upon your wisdom and strength. I must see my purpose. Reveal to me the secrets that the humanity of the south is holding," he whispered.

Dipping his hands into the cold water, he withdrew some of the blessed liquid in his palms and then brought it to his face. With a splash, he let the water flow over his eyes and cheeks before lowering his gaze to the rippling surface of the water.

Images of trees sprang up around the pool and a breeze cut through the clearing that stung his face with biting cold. He continued to stare, the images of trees shifting and beginning to fall, figures, men, bringing axe and fire to the forest.

This isn't what I seek… where is the son of the Hierophant?

The vision continued, ancient oak and towering pine were being felled as an army of mercenaries built siege towers around a green-stoned fortress. The keep was a rocky outcropping in a sea of trees so thick no light penetrated their canopy. Above the keep, a banner flew, one not unlike the emblems born by the heralds of men in the far north. The flag above the keep bore a rose field with a silver wand, and men in silvered helm stood along the crenellations, surveying the siege below.

Finally, Relan nodded, "I understand, Father, and I will see this tragedy diverted."

Clearing his mind of the vision, he leaned back and took a deep breath of cool, morning air. Winter was fast approaching and even in the south that meant cold nights and light snows.

If this siege is to take place, the day must be close at hand…

Rising to his feet, he collected his staff and turned to the west, as that was where his heart now told him to go.

Raising his hand, he prayed for aid, the staff held aloft in his other fist.

> *"Sing the song of morning*
> *Sing the song of night*
> *Come to me oh gentle wing*
> *I sorely need your sight"*

Kneeling in a bow, face to the earth, he whispered, "Oak Father, bless me with thy power," concluding his prayer.

Wind circled above the clearing surrounding the well, and within another moment a starling sailed in low and landed gracefully on Relan's outstretched palm.

"We must speak," Relan whispered.

The black bird cocked its shiny head and stared at him.

"Listen carefully to the wood. There is an army of men moving under its boughs, and I must know where it is," Relan said, "Repeat this message to others of your kind, and return to be my guide."

The bird chirped once before taking flight and disappearing into the skeletal trees beyond the ring of stones.

Birds make wonderful companions to a lone walker in the woods, and they can be very useful for vision questing, but harnessing the power of an entire flock... well birds are fast, and I'll know soon enough if my request was understood.

The sun waned thin and pale by midday and he could hear the sounds of a hunt growing louder through the thickets. Relan stopped among a stand of chestnut and closed his eyes.

Do you come for me or for bigger game?

He sniffed the air and then placed his staff against a tree. Pulling back his hood, he whispered words as he held both hands aloft. The air stirred and the branches above clicked against each other.

From the heart
the forest has blood
Bring to me its youth
so that I may have favor

From the tangles beyond the chestnut clutch a young buck appeared in the small clearing, his horns sharpened and his coat creamy brown and unblemished.

Relan raised his hand and waited as the deer came closer. Its black nose was wet from the chase and each heavy breath sent a small cloud of mist into the air, even in the relative heat of the afternoon. He reached forward and touched its head, the beast's ears falling back and one hoof stamping at the leaf-strewn ground.

"Time catches us all, my friend, and this day you serve the Oak Father in a way very few of your kind are able."

The deer twitched but didn't move. Relan reached within the folds of his wood-ring vest and drew forth a short-bladed knife. A sharp edge resided on a single side and the blade was thick with a tangle of runes etched into the metal.

He drew close to the deer, his mouth coming to its folded ear as he whispered a prayer, the knife pushing forward into the hollow of the creature's neck. It whined, but he held it by the snout and whispered further until its front legs gave out and he laid it gently upon the ground.

Kneeling beside it, he closed its eyes and began his work, the knife taking the creature apart as though it were made of parchment. He drew holly from a pouch at his side and waved it over the kill whispering more words before he cut pieces of hide into strips and tied large pieces of the animal to low-hanging branches.

He was quick, purposeful, his muscles straining to haul the meat, and his hands steady as he painted runes upon the trees in the beast's blood. Once finished he cleaned the knife and drew his hands through the leaves until the blood was replaced with a rich-brown dirt.

"Accept my scent among the trees, great Lowl, and the gift I offer," he said.

He heard no answering call, only the wind slipping through the trees and an occasional birdsong. After a moment's pause, he turned to leave the clearing, moving west, ever westward toward the sea. Only then did he hear a long howl, and this time much closer than before…

CHAPTER SEVEN

ERIK

*W*hat? *Just because you're watching me doesn't mean I've got to be noble of spirit. I mean, maybe you're watching me because I'm not the chivalrous type and therefore if I did do something honest and nice you'd stop watching all together...*

I'm not so different than everyone else. I've got needs, sometimes dark thoughts, notions of being greater than I am... all that kind of stuff. If you're a god, maybe you don't get what I'm saying, but if you're not, then I hope you have some inkling of understanding. We make what we can from the circumstances we're given, at least that's what my old master, Shera, used to say. You know Shera? Well, you should because she makes Anais look like a one-toothed beggar...

Damnit! Now you have me thinking about things better left alone, and a bit turned on to boot... Just follow me to Mahe, from there we can find our next road, assuming you're still interested...

The first watch was just settling in when Tavalori nudged Erik.

"Delvers," he whispered.

The word snapped him out of his sleep and Erik rose to help Tavalori wake the others. The area around the rise was a sea of mist that drifted across the marshes around the fallen tower. Light from the Ghost Moon shown silver in the tall grass as shapes moved like black spirits in the fen.

Raziel drew close to Erik's ear saying, "There must be half a hundred of them."

"What do we do against so many?" Telluria asked.

Erik got to his feet and marched to the horses. The two beasts drew hard against their tethers with ears rolled back and eyes wide.

"Two of you can still be away. The horses are tired but they'll carry you swiftly from this place. If you press them, you can still be in Mahe well before dawn."

Raziel stepped forward and reached for the reins, "Thank you. If we see anyone on the road, we will send them back to help you."

Erik grabbed the reins and raised an eyebrow, "The two people I was referring to were Anais and Telluria."

"Those are our horses!" Raziel spat, his hand going to the hilt of his blade.

Heat bloomed between the two, and the steeds grew wilder. Malcolm stepped in behind Raziel, and Tavalori nocked an arrow in his bow.

Erik held up a hand, "These are women, and you would leave one here? It'll not be an easy death they face at the hands of these creatures. You understand what happened to Telluria's mistress? It will be no less brutal for either of them here."

"Anais must make it safely to Mahe, and, without me…" Raziel began, but the young songstress stepped forward between the bristling warriors.

"Your argument is moot as I'm staying here. If you wish to turn tail and run, Raziel, then take the horses and ride from here with Telluria," she said.

Raziel looked to have been struck a physical blow, "You cannot be serious, my lady, you're…?"

Anais visibly stiffened and spat, "I'll not leave these men to die here. I've been trained in combat, and they will need every blade in the coming conflict." She continued in a whisper that nevertheless carried to Erik's ears, "and do not refer to me in such terms again!"

Telluria piped up too, "And every spell! I may be only an apprentice, but I can still command magic. I only hid from the last attack because my mistress demanded it but she is no longer here, so I may choose my own path this time."

Erik looked at them both and shook his head.

Foolish romantics… you've no idea what true combat is like, or the tortures that will befall you when you're finally pulled down… but do as you will, it's no cause of mine…

"Fine," Erik said.

He untied the reins of the two horses and tossed them to Raziel. The weight of the two beasts pulled the big man away until he was forced to release them. Like thundering shades, the horses fled down the opposite slope away from the Delvers.

Erik turned to the group, "Braxus, Malcolm, go see what is behind those stone arches at the base of the tower and what defense they can provide. We must find a way to channel the Delvers away from our flanks and force them to do battle with us one by one. And keep quiet, right now we are at the advantage, so I want to keep it that way."

Malcolm nodded at Braxus, and the two men rushed quietly up to the fallen tower. Behind them, Ash walked and chanted, his whispers too quiet to hear, but his path twisted among random stones, his little fingers touching some and spreading dust on others.

Erik turned to Telluria, "I need you behind any wall that protects you while also giving you a clear line of sight. Tavalori, you go with her. She's your responsibility and from her side your bow will be of greater use."

Tavalori shook his head, "I can fight up front."

The young man's eyes went to Anais and Erik sighed, "I am sure you can. But for the beginning of the battle we need your bow, not your blade, so do as I say."

Tavalori nodded grudgingly.

"And what of me?" Anais asked.

"You're coming with me," Raziel said, taking her arm and pulling her toward the downward slope away from the Delvers.

With a quick turn, she slapped Raziel so hard it brought tears to his eyes.

"You forget yourself!" she said.

Heat washed the top of the hill and Raziel's hand dropped to his blade, but Erik caught his eye with a shake of his head and the man breathed out a long calming breath.

"As you will," Raziel muttered.

Erik pointed to the fallen tower, "Anais, you'll hold the line with Malcolm, Braxus, and I."

"And me," Raziel stated flatly.

"Anais, go to Malcolm. He'll have a place for you. Raziel and I will bring up the rear." he finished.

Anais nodded and ran up the hill to the others. They watched her go, waiting until she had reached the others before turning back to face one another. Waves of heat spilled out between them and Erik let his fingers drop to the hilt of *Fury*. The movement brought both blades from their scabbards, Erik stepping back as Raziel did the same.

Erik spoke first, "Look, I know she's a high-born. What I don't know is what she's doing out here in the wilderness all by herself, or what your relationship is to her."

"It's none of your concern," Raziel replied.

"But it is. If you're her protector, then why let her stay? If she's nobility, then why no greater escort? There's something foul about the two of you, and what power she holds over you to take such abuse, I know not. That kind of intrigue makes me twitchy, and in this battle I can't afford any blades at my back."

"Mercenaries should be concerned with sword-work, and leave the business of strangers to themselves." Raziel said.

Erik smiled, "The more you protest, the more I want to slip this blade into you."

"I invite you to try," Raziel said.

"Speak up, or we can die here together because I'll hold you to this spot in defense until the Delvers take us both," Erik said.

Raziel's lips curled and his eyes looked into the dark fens then back again.

"She's a merchant's daughter and I've been hired to see her through Aflyr, but if I want my gold for the service I've got to do as she says," Raziel answered.

Liar… you'd get no gold if she's dead and yet you still put her at risk, but what reward is truly in that for you?

Erik let the tip of *Fury* fall slightly, saying, "Very well, then let's see that all fellow sell-swords come out of this battle, eh?"

Raziel nodded, "Agreed, for the journey we're allies."

Still a good distance apart, the two of them walked up the rise, the silhouette of the tower touched by the silver light of the Ghost Moon.

This night is going to be long and deadly and the last thing I need is a new-found enemy close enough to slip a blade into my back…

Erik watched from the tower wall as a Delver slunk into view. From the top of the tower's only remaining plateau, Tavalori raised his bow and let loose an arrow into the night. The lead Delver scout slumped and laid still, but Tavalori was already nocking another arrow before letting it fly, killing the next scout who came into view moments behind the first.

Keep them blind as long as we can… Erik thought.

He slipped up next to Telluria. She smelled of salt and foamy brine.

"What can you do?" he asked.

She took a deep breath, "Kill them."

"Excuse me?"

Tavalori let another arrow go, but this time there was a grunt followed by a guttural shout.

"That's done it," Braxus called up from below.

Erik looked over the lip of the wall, dark shapes now creeping in greater numbers up the rise. Telluria was still watching him when he ducked back below the wall. Water glistened on her lips and her hair was wet and hung about her pale face in dark lines.

"Ok," he began. "What exactly do you mean 'kill them'?"

"If they're within a certain radius, I'm sure I can destroy them, assuming… Well, as long as I am able to maintain control over the power of the *afterglow* that I hold, but I'll only have a single shot."

He looked back over the wall, the Delvers were growing closer, shields raised to ward against further shots by Tavalori. Reaching down, he pulled her up next to him and pointed down the hill. His touch drew a sharp breath from Telluria and gooseflesh along his arm.

"Can you clear them there? Force them to move toward the old entrance stones?" he asked.

She nodded, her eyes fixing on the spot. Erik snapped his hand away from her, a spark lighting his fingers as she drew on her power.

He looked down to Braxus and the others. "Ash, are the stones you enchanted dangerous?"

"If they get close enough," Ash smiled.

"Good, then be ready."

Telluria closed her eyes, her hands weaving through the air and the hair on the back of Erik's neck standing on end. Beyond the stones Delvers started to blow horns, battle platoons forming up for the final charge into the ruin.

"Arms!" Erik yelled.

The enemy readied shields and cast visors down over eyes while Erik whispered a prayer for luck to his feline goddess and unsheathed *Fury*. Then the world shuddered as though struck by a mighty blow. As he looked on, a blast of light exploded in the sky that turned night into day.

An enormous ball of white-fire blossomed like a lotus out from the main mass of Delvers, the braying of their horns instantly dying as *after-glow* magic ripped the landscape apart. His breath caught in his throat as he glimpsed the carnage and chaos filling the field.

"By the gods..." Erik whispered.

Beside him Telluria slumped against his shoulder, her skin wet and water dripping from her long hair. He caught her, the stink of elemental water so powerful his spark cooled and he shook to the bone.

Horns began to blow again, the Delvers were regrouping on the trail below. Once more they pressed forward. Erik held Telluria against his chest, heart pounding as he blinked away the threads of spark-snuffing unconsciousness that pulled at him.

Don't black out, keep her water at bay... it will subside...

At the outer edge of the ruin, among the fallen stones, another explosion shook the hill, this time one of Ash's making. Fire rose thirty feet in the sky and Ash laughed and danced like a demon below the tower.

"Burn you devils!" the Eldaryn screamed.

From within the flame, shadows loomed, Delvers in heavy plate and trailing smoke lumbered out of the flames with an aura of earth sheathing them.

"They've got a shaman!" Malcolm called.

The smell of freshly tilled earth enveloped the tower and Erik leaned Telluria gently against the wall to get a better view. Beside him Tavalori still had his bow at the ready.

"I don't see anything," Tavalori said.

"Neither do I, but something is enhancing their element, empowering their defense."

Below the sound of combat broke like a wave among the rocks, Braxus spouting out a series of curses. Erik tapped Tavalori on the shoulder, "Keep watch, the shaman will have to appear and when he does see that he's dealt with."

Tavalori nodded and Eric leapt down what remained of the wooden stair, a collection of Delvers already hammering away at the tower's small defense. Erik brought *Fury* up and clove the hand off of a Delver who was trying to flank the party's shield phalanx by climbing over the wall.

"Malcolm?" Erik yelled.

"Yeah?"

"How many?"

It was Raziel who answered, "Ten here, but they won't fall, the earth's keeping them up."

Erik leapt onto the four-foot wall, the remaining Delvers mustered at the tower entrance surged against Malcolm and Braxus's shields but Raziel's blade kept them back as he used it like a spear between the two warrior's defenses.

Beyond them a dozen Delver bodies still burned amid the stones and the night mist clung heavy to the fens at the base of the hill. A Delver marked him and moved away from the bottleneck, Erik jumping to the ground engaging it before it took the high ground.

Fury clashed against its hammer, the thing also swinging with its shield as it drove Erik back and away from the wall.

Keep your calm, it's just a single Delver...

He parried another blow, the Delver lurching forward as an arrow found purchase in the base of its neck. Erik brought *Fury* down and clove the thing's helm in two, brains and earthly stink spilling out before he backed away.

Two more Delvers broke from the bottleneck, and Erik fell back toward the still steaming stones. He felt the heat, the fire in his chest rekindling as the first of the two brutes engaged him. He ducked behind a stone, the Delver's scimitar biting deep and sending chips in all directions.

The second Delver was on him from the other side, *Fury* coming up to turn the blade before the creature's shield caught him in the face. His helm rang like a bell, and he stumbled back into the charred grass. He rolled, came up and swung, *Fury* striking the leg armor of an attacker as the second one turned away from him with a sliding stagger.

Anais was there, her rapier broken in half and a look of shock on her face. The Delver took a staggering step toward her, the end of Anais's blade protruding from its back, but an arrow suddenly lodged itself between the slits in the thing's facemask and it tumbled down at her feet.

Erik brought *Fury* up again, his spark flaring, as he turned the Delver's scimitar and reposted back across his body in a stroke that slit the creature's neck. Blood wetted the earth and Erik stepped past the dying Delver to grab Anais by the arm and pull her behind a stone.

"Are you crazy?" he demanded.

She blinked twice, "It was like sticking a bag of dirt..."

He slapped her and she let out a slight scream but her eyes refocused. Hissing, he pressed his lips close her ear, "If you want to live, pay attention."

Heat burned between them, but she said nothing.

"Our defense won't hold them forever, and I need to find their shaman. Without him their earthly resistance will fail." He shook her then, "Do you understand?"

She nodded. He pulled a skinning knife from his belt and handed it to her.

"It's not much use against Delvers, but if things turn bad I suggest taking it to your own throat. It's sharp and will make it quick."

He pulled away but he could still feel her fire on his heels as they moved down the slope, the smell of earth strong in his nostrils.

Keep up your spell, shaman, because I'll follow the scent of it right to you...

His boots touched water but he waded in, the cold bog sucking at his heels until he heard a voice drifting through the mist.

"There," Anais whispered.

He followed her pointing finger and on a small rise among the grass he saw a figure rocking back and forth with head down.

"Stay here," he said.

"No."

Erik turned and Anais was so close to his face he could have kissed her without moving. She smelled of lilacs and honey, her heat making his blood boil.

"I'm coming with you. If this shaman doesn't die, then all of us will, so we have to be sure."

He paused only a moment and then turned back to the figure. His feet sloshed in the water, but the shaman's murmuring covered the sound until he was close enough to make out the lines of age and strange tattoos on the Delvers tan face.

It looked up and he sprang, *Fury* falling down like the blade of a guillotine. The shaman waved a hand and a wall of earth sprang up, *Fury* biting deep into it but not penetrating.

He pulled the blade free and swung again, this time *Fury's* cross-cut split the earthen wall but the shaman was chanting again. The enemy's eyes rolled back and earth-stink saturated the island when Anais sprang from within the rushes on the far side of the mound and plunged her dagger hilt-deep into the creature's side.

The earth smell was sucked away like water from a upturned bottle and Erik took advantage, *Fury* reaching out to disembowel the Delver where he stood clutching the dagger in his ribs. Entrails poured onto the ground and he fell forward until his face lay at the water's edge.

Anais stood breathing heavily, and Erik approached her with a thin smile.

"That was brave," he said.

She looked up at him, "And needed. Next time, don't be such an arrogant fool as to think you don't need me."

She pushed past him and marched back into the water. He watched her go, the fire in his gut burning hot before he followed. Ahead, a horn blew the call for a retreat among the remaining Delvers.

She surprises me again, and with Mahe less than a day away my decisions become no easier…

CHAPTER EIGHT

ERIK

Back again I see… I really must be important or you're way too concerned with my love life. Perhaps you're a love god, or better yet a goddess. Now that would be interesting.

Gods! I am not getting anywhere with Anais, you'd think that seducing a mere woman would be easier than fighting off a large band of Delvers, but, NO! And worse, now I've a cold-fleshed water witch flirting with me. Part of me just wants to ditch this motley band and strike out on my own. But then there is that pressing feeling that I need to stay here, as if the weight of the world depends on it. Stupid, I know. I could have seduced half a dozen tavern wenches with the work it takes to just get a little smile out of her. I need to rethink my strategies with that one…

Raziel sounded a bit piggy when he breathed. The bandages on his face were doing their best to keep his nose in place. The bodyguard came away the most heavily injured from the fight, a Delver hammer having caught him in the face and shattering his helm.

Erik walked beside the large man, a hand extended to steady him as he walked.

"We're almost to the city," Erik said.

Raziel nodded, the entire company now walking with the horses lost in the fen. Ahead, farmsteads dotted the rolling landscape but most appeared deserted, with livestock gone and chimneys unlit.

"I know it's late in the season, but you'd think there would be more signs of life," Malcolm said.

Erik nodded, "True, it makes me wonder if last night's Delver attack was not an isolated incident."

"If so, this might be a precursor to an attack from The Broken Land," Malcolm said.

Braxus shook his head, "In winter? That makes no sense."

"I agree, there's definitely something going on. The countryside shouldn't be this deserted, especially so close to the gates of Mahe, ," Erik said.

Ahead, the walls of the city rose up on the horizon, towers dark against the backdrop of mountains to the north, their cliffs touched with the first snows of the season. White seabirds drifted on the breeze and somewhere inside the city a bell rang.

Erik looked behind him, Tavalori and Ash walking with the two ladies, the Eldaryn's voice rising and falling as he told yet another story of his ne'er-do-well god. Anais caught his eye, and her look hardened, as she turned back toward Tavalori, she linked her arm through his and leaned in far closer than necessary.

Wonderful… he thought.

"There are no patrols either, and I see only the city banner upon the battlements," Malcolm said.

Erik turned back, the walls growing more distinct with every step.

"Braxus, how many free companies are in Mahe?" he asked.

"At least half a dozen, not to mention the city guard and two knightly orders," Braxus answered.

"If the banners are gone, that means the companies are gone as well, so who's defending the city?" Malcolm asked.

Erik shook his head, "I guess we'll find out soon enough."

The streets of Mahe were empty, strikingly empty, considering it was the greatest western sea port of the Aflyrian Empire. In the harbor only small fishing vessels and coastal sloops were in dock, and the wall garrison that allowed the company through the south gate looked far too thin and young to have pulled more than a season of duty.

Mahe was old, even by the standards of the south. Her streets were rutted and grooved, her walls pitted sandstone, and her architecture dominated by marble columns and green copper roofs.

The sea and time had taken its toll on the city, but the greatness of it still shown in the mighty Clerical District and the Merchant Quarter where mansions were commonplace. The city's verdigris roofs were known far and wide, and sailors called Mahe the Jade Labyrinth, as a man could get lost in its thin twisting streets.

Fog had collected along the docks by the time they reached them. The layer of gloom around the marina was magnified by the blood red glow that permeated the ancient Mahian Palace on the northern hill of the city.

"Why does the palace glow?" Ash asked.

"It's cursed," Anais replied. "That crimson stain kills anything it touches, and the castle has stood inside that deadly light for a thousand years."

Ash stared at the palace, the towers framed by the mountains to the north, "How is that possible?"

"Wizards," Erik said.

He didn't look back at Telluria, instead pulling Raziel away from the group and calling over his shoulder, "Find an inn on this main road, preferably close to this gate and I'll find you there once I've had the priests tend to Raziel."

Braxus followed him, the rest of the company trailing behind as Ash continued with his questions.

"They're an odd lot," Braxus said.

"You're one to talk…" Erik said.

Braxus laughed which was echoed by a burbled moan from Raziel.

"What do you make of the garrison?" Braxus asked.

"Bare bones, nothing but boys and old men. I don't understand it, and from the look, half the city is abandoned as well."

Braxus nodded, "But only recently I'd think because there doesn't appear to have been any looting or destruction."

"No banners, no guards, and little people… I'd say we've stepped into something here Braxus."

"All the better if you had thieving in mind."

Raziel moaned again, the blow having stripped from him any sense since the battle.

Erik looked toward the Clerical District, well-worn temples dominating a hill that shown with hundreds of massive lamps along war-sturdy retaining walls of grey granite.

"The temples still hold fire, so there'll be no golden relics for the easy picking," Erik said.

Braxus jingled his purse, "Coins are growing thin, my friend, and even with the chink we found on the Delvers, Raziel's wounds are going to cost us plenty."

"I know, but we've no choice."

Laughing, Braxus said, "There's always a choice, and this one looks pretty clear if you ask me."

Erik shook his head, "I don't know… I've got a feeling."

"That doesn't sound too promising, the last time you *had a feeling* Kaleb got killed and we had to flee Arcania on the evening tide."

Erik shrugged, "True, but we had plenty of gold for the ladies of Bandar Abbas when we landed."

They walked on, Braxus sucking at a yellowed tooth until he finally spoke, "Fine, but if anyone dies this time, it had better be Malcolm."

"Or this guy," Erik pointed a thumb at Raziel.

The minstrel moaned again but kept on going, the golden orbs of the Sun's Gods Temple the first to alight their path once they crossed the threshold to the holy hill.

The inn was a great marble structure, probably a grand stable during the height of the Aflyrian Empire, the pillars framing the once grand doors were carved in the shape of a pair of prancing stallions. A weathered sign hung on brass fittings above the door depicting a black fish and a rising wave.

Erik and Braxus stood outside, the misty cloak of night twining around them, the flame of a guttering lamp the only light falling on the slick cobbles.

"The third inn along the road… you'd think we'd have found them by now," Braxus said.

Erik nodded, his hand pushing open the smaller door cut within the larger carriage doors that were now sealed with heavy bands of wood above the pedestrian entry.

A warm and golden glow spilled out into the street, the mist blown back in swirls as the sound of pipes and laughter filled the air. The duo made their way into the common room, lamps smoking on wooden supports and two dozen tables set the hall around a central kitchen and bar.

"Smells good," Braxus said.

The odor of savory meat and the flavors of Ushan, Arcania, and even the T'ung set Erik's mouth to watering at the aroma. He smelled a hint of ginger in the air and an undercurrent of curry.

"There," Braxus pointed.

Erik followed the man's finger, a small gathering of city-folk stomping and drinking together as Anais spun among them. She had replaced her breeches with a flowing skirt and showcased her ample cleavage with an off the shoulder shirt and tightly laced bodice.

They played the crowd, Ash working the pipes and Anais chiming in here and there with a verse drown out by raucous laughter.

"This can't be good…" Erik said.

"I don't know. I see the shine of coins in the bag at the Leprechaun's feet."

Erik shook his head, "You've the eyes of a hawk, my friend."

They approached the throng, Anais seeing them and spinning down her dance before placing a hand on Ash's shoulder. As the little man let the last notes bleed out, the men around them called for more. The heat of so much humanity overwhelmed the presence of the great oven in the middle of the hall.

"Nay, gentlemen, that's it for me, but I thank you for your rousing accompaniment," Anais said.

Angry voices rose among the men but as Malcolm and Tavalori moved to stand behind Anais, the complaints dropped to a quiet murmur, and the group of patrons broke up, going back to their meals and conversations. Erik and Braxus pressed past those leaving, Anais catching Erik's eye before she turned and pressed herself against Tavalori's chest and whispered something in his ear.

Are you toying with me? All the times we have spoken you seem less than interested, and yet you let your gaze bore into me while pawing Tavalori? You play a dangerous game…

Erik took a seat, "Raziel will heal, but slowly, the damage was deeper than we suspected."

"Meaning what?" Telluria asked.

"Meaning he's not thinking right and the touch of the Sun God will take time to put his mind right," Erik said.

"How long?" Anais asked.

"A god's blessings are a strange and untimely thing, or so they told me," Erik answered.

Anais leaned against Tavalori's shoulder, her hair back and her face flushed and covered in a sheen of sweat.

"And what of the gates, did you investigate their lack of guard any further?" Malcolm asked.

Erik shook his head, "No, and I didn't report the Delvers either since I didn't feel like starting a panic."

"It still makes no sense," Anais said.

Tavalori agreed, saying, "The Fortress at Nehru is charged with the southern defense of Aflyr. That bastion should have caught a Delver force of that size before it made the western marshes or at least sent warning to the city that they had broken through."

"We just came from Nehru within the month and although sparsely garrisoned, it held the southern passes and no word of Delvers circulated among the men," Malcolm said.

"So how did they get this far north?" Telluria asked.

Malcolm shrugged, "Goat paths, a break in the Kin defense along the western shores... who knows."

A barmaid appeared at the table, pock-faced and thick with something of the Pagan League showing in her long nose. "What can I get for you?"

"Beer," Braxus said.

"And a hot plate for travelers weary from the road," Erik added.

"There's only Relo's Stew, skewered pork, bread, and some fried vegetables to go with the beer, but I can bring enough for the table."

"That's a sparse menu," Braxus said.

The barmaid nodded, "With the merchants gone and the tall ships having forgone the harbor, the city is managing on what we can get."

"Merchants gone?" Malcolm asked.

"Yep, and all the nobles, as of two weeks ago. Even the farmers have fled. Spices, meat, produce... everything is running low."

"This doesn't make any sense, even with the coming of the winter season," Anais said.

The barmaid nodded, "It's old King NyWinter. He put out the call to come to ChanderNagor and everyone who could left the city in a rush, many nobles taking the folk of the farmsteads and their animals along with them."

Anais's face grew pale. "NyWinter?" she asked.

"Indeed, and with what's left in the city to defend it, the locals are thanking the gods its winter because otherwise there might be a serious threat if the Delvers come raiding."

Those around the table exchanged dark looks and Ash said, "We just fought..."

Malcolm covered the Eldaryn's mouth, saying, "Bring what food you can, it'll be most welcome."

The barmaid furrowed a brow, but nodded and walked away. Malcolm pulled his hand from Ash's mouth with a curse and a shake.

"Gods! Are you made of fire?"

"I am when I'm mad."

Anais said, "We can't let her know there are Delvers a day south, she'll spread the news to every ear in the inn and then there will be panic."

"Agreed, but we need to tell someone because the gates aren't safe, especially if there's a larger force we haven't seen yet," Erik said.

"Perhaps a guard captain?" Tavalori suggested.

Malcolm nodded, "If a competent one still remains in the city."

"Well, something is going on, and if a King draws his nobility, army, and livestock from a city this size, it has to mean..." Telluria broke off.

Erik finished for her, "That he's given up the city and plans to hold off the enemy elsewhere."

They all mumbled agreement as the barmaid returned with heavy platters. The steaming bowls of stew quieted their conversation and the beer took the edge off their flaring sparks. The night wore on, the company finally breaking apart to retire to their respective rooms.

Erik stood in the courtyard adjoining the inn, his boots beside him and his naked feet burning prints in the dusting of snow that had fallen the night before. Above thick clouds hid the sun, their steel-grey hue turning the morning into a cold and bleak affair in the half-abandoned city.

He raised himself on his toes, dropped back to the cobbles in a crouch, and then ran at the single tree in the center of the square. His stride never wavered as he pressed one foot against the trunk, turned in the air, and propelled himself into the lower branches.

Heat bloomed from his legs during the spring, his fingers taking hold of a branch and his back muscles pulling him up in a single fluid extension. He sat on the limb a moment, then dropped down to a smaller one, hung a moment, then pulled himself up to chin level fifty consecutive times before he finally dropped to the ground.

"Impressive," Telluria said.

Erik spun around, his hand going to the knife he always kept strapped horizontally to the back of his belt along with a concealed wand from the days when he was with Shera.

Telluria stood against the entry arch, her brown robes now covered with a heavy cloak trimmed in fur that framed her face like a northern princess.

"You're an early riser too I see," Erik said.

His voice was dull and his breathing quick, as he retrieved his boots and shirt from where they lay.

"Not really, my roommate rose earlier than I and she woke me when she left," Telluria said.

"Where was she going?" Erik asked a little too sharply.

Telluria sighed, "She didn't say, but she seemed very pleased with herself."

I bet she did...

"How did you learn to do that?" Telluria asked.

"What?"

"Climb a tree in a single leap."

He shook his head, "I picked it up when I was a kid and decided to see if I could still do it."

"Do I look so naive? I bet you do that sort of thing quite regularly." she said.

He didn't answer but slipped on his shirt and walked toward her. She held her ground, the smell of sea salt present in the crisp morning air.

"It's none of your concern," he said.

"Unless I need something stolen... am I right to call you a second story man?"

He drew close to her, his heat tangling with her vapors creating a veil of steam around them in the shadow of the arch.

"That's a professional title better left unsaid in a city such as this," he hissed.

She leaned in bringing their faces even closer. He saw now that her eyes were a deep emerald green and her skin, normally a pale ivory, had turned the pale blue-green color of sea foam. He could just smell the sweet scent of honeysuckle breaking through her sea stink and it unnerved him.

"You're much more dangerous than you seem," she said.

He forced a smile, "Only when I'm cornered."

Ducking, he slipped past her, a tremor quaking in his stomach. His clothes and hair were soaked, boots squishing as he turned the corner to the main thoroughfare, Braxus almost running into him.

"Gods," Erik cursed. "What's the rush?"

Braxus was breathless, "Anais... where is she?"

Erik shrugged, Telluria's voice called out from behind him, "She left early."

"Bastards and bitches!" Braxus spat.

He started away when a cat screeched like a demon's call across the street followed quickly by the angry squawking of chickens. Braxus didn't hesitate, his long strides carrying him across the street as the door to a stable was thrown open, smoke billowing outward along with a shirtless Tavalori and a flush-faced Anais.

"Now that's something you don't see every day..." Erik said.

Telluria brushed up against him and his skin prickled. "I guess we know why she was so pleased with herself."

"Yeah... but why is Braxus so concerned about her comings and goings?"

Telluria didn't reply, just slipped past him and headed back toward the doors of the inn. Across the way Braxus was helping Anais back toward the inn as well, Tavalori still gasping for air as he cleared smoke from his lungs.

Looks like Anais has chosen Tavalori, which is probably better for me and to the Nine Hells with her anyway, but the bigger question is what's with Braxus's new obsession with her?

Looking back toward the inn he caught sight of Telluria as she slipped inside and a moment later a small shadow with orange hair followed.

Yep... I really don't want to know what Ash has to do with this either...

Spiced potatoes steamed on a central platter and thick slices of ham sat on each plate around the table. Sweet mead and three loaves of bread sat with the rest, Erik knifing some potatoes and adding them to his plate.

"I'm no sage, nor do I care to be, but I'd still like to hear more of the legion," Erik said.

Telluria sat beside him, a steaming cup of dark tea between her slender fingers.

"It's an old tale, one I'm sure most children of Aflyr are told. Simply stated, a thousand years ago, when the last free King of Mahe, Quin Imperus, still ruled the West of Aflyr, a court Wizard named Hafra Elim cursed the palace and king's legendary Axis Legion using powerful binding spells.

"Elim was a member of the Order of Towers, and a master of the necromantic arts. He bound his service to King Imperus for the price of the king's youngest daughter. For a decade the Ebon Robe served the king and did his bidding to secure the lands of the Aflyrian West and the city of Mahe from the encroaching dominance of the NyWinter King of Eastern Aflyr.

"When the time at last arrived for the princess to be married to the Wizard, the king cast off the bargain. Imperus's intent was to marry his daughter to the young King Axos Ergoroth of Lystbrook and form a powerful alliance with the forest kingdom to the northwest."

Erik took a long drought of his beer, "Again, what does this have to do with us?"

"Yeah," Braxus agreed.

Telluria sighed, "You said the city was in jeopardy."

"So?"

"So you need to hear me out. You may think me only an apprentice but I've been studying history for a century longer than anyone in the company has been alive."

The table quieted, Telluria taking a sip from her tea before she continued.

"After the breaking of the contract, Elim seethed and stormed about the palace but the king paid little notice. During a night of dark contemplation, Elim supposedly used his own body to create a Portal of Damnation inside the Palace of Mahe, freezing the Axis Legion as they slept and surrounding the palace grounds with a deadly and impenetrable red glow.

"It's said that without his army, the king and his entire family were slain by Elim, before the spell at last consumed him. As you can see, even today a scarlet glow still surrounds the northern Palace of Mahe on its walled hill. People have often written tales telling of the damned legion that slumbers on inside the crimson stained walls of the palace" she finished.

"Do you believe the tale?" Anais asked.

Telluria sat a long moment before she replied, "Although such a thing is far beyond even my late mistress to conceive, I know the spells of stasis are powerful tools, as are demon-born curses, and almost anything is possible for the upper orders of magic. If Elim made a pact for his own soul with a demon or greater power to bind all the men of the king so he could then use his skills for a bloody vengeance, that tale might hold more truth than many realize."

"Then we have to free them and save the city," Anais said.

Malcolm coughed and Braxus started shaking his head.

Raising an eyebrow Erik said, "What makes you so willing to help?"

"Because I'm …" she trailed off.

After a pause, Ash finished her sentence, "A princess."

All eyes looked first to the priest and then to Anais.

"How?" she whispered.

"Bandylegs told Braxus and I the truth about her in a dream," Ash said.

Erik looked at Braxus, then back to Anais, "Although that answer has several more questions laced in it, I think the most pressing one I have is Princess of what?"

"Lystbrook…" Anais said.

"Then you're Igrayn, daughter of King Ergoroth of Lystbrook," Malcolm said. "But what are you doing out in Aflyr posing as a minstrel?"

"That's none of your business," Anais/Igrayn answered.

"It is if you expect our help defending Mahe, which in all reality still isn't any of our concerns," Malcolm said.

Erik felt the heat rolling off of Igrayn, saw Malcolm and Braxus leaning back in their chairs and a confused expression formed on Tavalori's face.

"Nobility is pressed with a responsibility to all people, even those of a foreign nation," she said. "Besides, once I am married, I will be Queen of this realm, so they will be my responsibility soon enough."

Erik laughed, "That is a new definition of noble to me, as I always thought it meant you get to take what you want, when you want it and to hell with the common man."

"You, sir, are like every common man my instructors warned me about."

"Truly?" Erik asked.

"Yes, there's no spirit in you, just a shine of greed and self-service."

Malcolm broke in, "Sounds like she's discovered the true you, Erik."

"Indeed," Erik said.

"Wait, then that makes Raziel your…" Tavalori asked.

"My knight defender from the Citadel of the Moon," Igayn answered.

"Then he should be the one you're talking to about saving Mahe," Braxus said.

The heat off Igrayn was palpable, but she smiled politely and nodded. Erik raised a hand, saying, "We have no true knowledge of when Raziel will be well enough to leave the healing beds of the temple, and with the Delvers lurking, there's no time to waste."

She cast Erik a questioning look, saying, "Then we'll have to enter the palace without him."

"Enter what palace?" Malcolm asked.

"*The* palace. If the city is truly defenseless and left as bait or fodder for an invading force then I intend to do what I can to save it. If the only option is following a legend, then so be it," Igrayn answered.

Erik took another drink of his mead before he sighed, staring hard at Igrayn. "If you really want me to go, then I'll do it."

Malcolm and Braxus both made strangled noises in their throats.

"You're serious?" Igrayn asked.

Erik nodded, "Well, I couldn't have you going back to Lystbrook believing all common men are so base in their motivations."

Igrayn smiled and stood, "Good, then I'll be off to check on Raziel before we settle on a plan."

Tavalori was on his feet almost as quickly, "I'll accompany you."

"As will I," Ash added.

Igrayn looked like she would protest but Ash beat her to the door. Once the trio had cleared out, Malcolm spoke. "This is foolishness, Erik."

"True, but I feel I need to help these people," Erik said.

Malcolm shook his head and made a grunting noise, "You wish to help yourself to a Princess of Lystbrook if you ask me."

"I think the young Tavalori is already hot on that game trail," Erik said.

"You could have her if you wanted, and I'd say she's ripe for the plucking now that her shield knight is laid low," Malcolm replied.

"That's not in the cards," Braxus said.

The both looked at him, Erik asking, "Do tell, Braxus, and speak also of sharing dreams with a Leprechaun."

Braxus shook his head, "The priest is mistaken."

"I might agree, save your frantic search for the then unmasked princess this morning," Erik said.

"I was simply holding up a promise I made to Raziel before we left the houses of healing."

Erik shook his head, "You only make promises you keep when there's something in it for you."

Braxus shrugged but said no more. Beside him Malcolm stabbed another heap of potatoes, saying, "I just hope there will be coin in it for us. Saving a city is a noble deed, but looting a fallen palace is much more in my line of work."

"I guess we'll just have to see what happens on the morrow," Erik replied.

Streets loomed up out of the morning light, frost settling on stones and roofs with long white fingers. The company, dressed for war, stood under the cloud-heavy sky at the base of the hill that the once grand palace stood upon.

Todmann, Lead Healer of the Sun Temple, stood with them, his eyes raised and a prayer on his lips. He was tall, well over six feet with thick brown hair and a stout mustache. He wore amber robes over chainmail, carried a studded mace at his hip and sported a jade talisman around his neck.

"Good Priest, what do you make of it?" Anais asked.

"I prayed on your plight last night. The fate of Mahe was shown to me in a spiritual revelation by the light of the dawn. I knew my course would be to assist you in any way I could, but the glowing curse is daunting nonetheless," Todmann answered.

"Well, *Igrayn*," Erik emphasized the name. "I'd say we don't have a fig's chance in the Abyss of getting in there, I mean look at the rats."

Several feet on either side of the glow were rat corpses, some little more than bone and fur while others looked fresh within the hour.

"I mark it as no damn good," Braxus said.

The mercenary held a Delver axe in one hand and his broadsword in the other.

"Agreed," Erik said.

"There has to be some other way in," Igrayn said.

"Perhaps there is," Todmann said. "Indeed, it's as you say, that for a thousand years nothing has been able to penetrate the glow, but that doesn't mean there haven't been people who've entered the palace."

"Meaning?" Malcolm asked.

"You see, I wasn't always a priest. In my youth, I, like so many other children in this city, was a homeless urchin. As I grew, I spent time with other wild youths, stealing food and coppers, playing games of swords and stones, and also finding pathways around the city other than the guarded streets.

"It was in my fourteenth winter that I heard the rumor of the storm sewer that led under the hill and into the half-sunken chambers below the old palace. Although I wasn't foolish enough to go into that tunnel myself, I had friends who did. Some of them returned with gold coins and tales of lurking creatures, while others were never heard from again."

Erik sucked at his bottom lip, "Do you remember where the entrance is?"

"I do."

"And you've seen it with you own eyes?" Erik asked.

"I have, and I will do more than simply show it to you. As a sun priest it's my duty to see this city protected, be it from Delver raiders *or* treasure-seeking looters. I will go with you," Todmann said, eyeing them all keenly.

Erik cast a sidelong glance to Malcolm, "Agreed, we wouldn't want to see the city betrayed."

"Then let's be away, the day and the Delvers wait not for us," Igrayn said.

Todmann nodded and led the party up the street, Erik lagging behind, his eyes watching the glow and the shadowed palace rising beyond.

CHAPTER NINE

RELAN

*D*o you see? The forest provides and the hunt has ended before the coming of the Ghost Moon. Now I walk the day without pursuit and yet you trail me as always, watching for something I cannot understand.

Is it a tale you seek? Is it knowledge of this current quest or something from the past that might quench your thirst and send you elsewhere?

What strange need can I, a simple servant of the Hierophant and the Oak Father, cause in one so utterly mysterious?

Know you that I was once a man, a water-born and gifted Wizard in the lands of the New Kingdoms, trained by immortals in the Towers? I served a king and painted destruction with my talents until I succumbed to the oldest of enemies… the telltale heart.

I cast about my Order like a ship blown in a gale, I threw down my mantel of service to kings and took the call of the necromancer and the powers of death… but my power spilled out of me with each troubled beating of my heart at the loss of a love I couldn't have.

When I fell it was to lesser things, simple creatures that hunted me like a feral animal among the woods, my power broken and my life spent.

The Hierophant found me then, or what remained, and drew a new body and healthy spirit from the clay. My water spark was replaced with the shared passions of fire and the longevity of air.

So I am a druid reborn and my memory of a fallen life is only shadow-stuff among the ruins of my mind.

Have I satisfied you? Will you now depart?

No… I feel you still, and so I will continue forward as always, but stay back for the power of life and death comes to me on the breeze and I must soon decide what to do with it…

Relan looked to the sky as the first wisps of snow came trailing down from the iron-colored clouds.

A troubled day lies ahead…

He walked on, the path rising over another hill to the west as his tattered green cloak fluttered behind him. To the east, the Wintertide spilled out in a sea of brown and spotted olive, and the towers of steam and hidden glens of the deep interior were forgotten beyond the horizon.

Finally he stopped as the clinking of armor and the stomping of many feet drifted over the rise. With a wave, he drew his cloak around him, and lowered himself to a kneeling position beneath a stand of pines.

From that position he whispered words to his deity.

"Changing Seasons
Skies refreshed
Mask of nature
Cover my flesh"

The color of his skin and clothing shifted until he was more plant than man among the grey and brown of the forest. Above, the snow continued to fall and he saw men moving through the basin of the mighty glen with drawn cloaks and heavy mantles.

They were costal humans, heat streaming from them as they walked in metal-shod boots, dingy mail, and pointed helms. The foot soldiers wore stout blades and carried spears half-again their height and among them road cavalry with steel-tipped lances and the livery of knights. At their head rode men in plate, a banner held aloft bearing the jade field and golden kingfisher of Lystbrook.

There is no elder king at the head but instead a young man… The prince perhaps but what is he doing so deep within the sacred wood?

Heavily armored commanders and sub-lieutenants drove the soldiers forward. The army paid little attention to the foliage in their path, slashing and trampling anything in their way. The force followed a small horse-trail that twisted up the glen toward a castle at the far end of the natural deep. It was a great and ancient thing, the towers tall and square, the thick walls dark with the stains of a thousand seasons.

Staying well back from their flank, he walked the trail behind them for hours. When evening broke he again ascended the hills seeking a place to sleep for the night. The wind howled from the heights, and he looked down from the summit to watch hundreds of cooking fires cast smoke into the growing gloom of dusk.

He found a spot to bed down among an outcropping of stone, his body shielded by a collection of rocks that cut the wind and concealed his presence. Reaching into his cloak he withdrew a leaf-wrapped piece of venison from yesterday's kill and laid it on the ground. Snow had already gathered in little patches among the rocks and he brushed some into his hands before depositing it on another leaf before him.

"Oak Father, provider of all things, bring forth what bounty you may bestow on this meager servant so that I might continue to do your bidding..." he prayed.

Amid the leaves a collection of cave mushrooms, onion, and shelled nuts appeared.

He withdrew a shock of holly and waved it over the bounty before he brought the tip of his staff down toward the meat. The trio of phoenix there blazed to life and soon the meat began to sizzle. Savory aromas rose from the roasting flesh that brought saliva running to his mouth.

Waving the staff over the nuts he waited until they cracked and steamed in the cold of dusk. The snow he'd collected was melting and he whispered words that cupped the leaves around it and bound them with magic until they formed a drinking vessel.

"A bounty indeed," he said, contentedly.

He ate in peace, his fingers slick with grease by the time his stomach was full. Silently thanking the oak father for his repast, he drew his staff close and wrapped his cloak about his shoulders.

The Hierophant of Cabal once told me that death was a part of life, but such a statement is easy to make if you've lived four thousand years and have no threat to your existence. The men below are simple folk, some certainly with families, and all dedicated to their own survival in the natural order...

From far below, the smell of Dravarian coffee, roasting meat, and beer drifted up the heights to where he sat.

Druids are meant to stand upon the middle ground, but tomorrow I'll have to make a decision that takes me a step away from neutrality…

A song drifted up to him, the men making merry amid the cold and dark that closed in around them.

What could be happening in Lystbrook? Why would the Ergoroth Prince bring a force into the Wintertide this late in the season? They'd have to know such a course would go against the natural order of the forest and put their men in jeopardy…

Leaning back, he looked into the clear night sky, the stars twinkling down. Below, the sound of laughter drifted through the cold night until sleep took him.

Dreams troubled his sleep and he woke as the Blood Moon eclipsed the silver light of the Ghost Moon and bled its crimson glow down into the trees.

The camp was quiet. Relan picked up his staff and made his way down the slope. Renewing the mimic enchantment, he slipped through a line of drowsy-eyed pickets with arms wrapped around spears.

The camp stank of humanity, the collective heat of their number causing the light snow to melt as it fell on the ground where they slept. He passed their sleeping bodies, amid cloak, blanket, and fur until the tents of the knights loomed like red flowers under the moon.

Guards here were more alive, eyes bright and spears held forward.

Relan knelt to the ground, ran a hand over the dirt and closed his eyes.

"From the tunnels
and from the earth
I ask for the shape
That scurries below."

The guard turned toward the sound, his spear dropping into a two-handed grip and his boots squishing the waterlogged leaves. A rat scurried away from him and he gave a harrumph before returning to his post.

Relan drew himself up, his perspective odd and disorienting until he shook himself and found his focus.

Rats are ever the common companion to humanity, and now to see what secrets hide within these tents…

He moved forward, paws cold on the ground until he slipped beneath the first canvas flap. Inside men snored and a single lamp burned at a low level. Jumping among the bedclothes, he found only elder men and slipped out the far side to the next tent.

This one held more light, and his black eyes blinked as he entered beneath the wall. A man lay upon several blankets, his lower body naked as another man waved his hands over him and chanted.

Beside the pair an older human in fine livery sat on a stool, his eyes sunken and his beard unkempt.

"How much longer?" the man in blankets asked.

"Rest, my prince, the priest must work his magic," the seated man said.

"I tire of this daily ritual and I tire of the gods that delay my healing," the prince said.

"Healing is not a perfect magic, and a man without these blessings of the hand of the gods would be laid in a bed all winter after the blow you took in the stable."

The prince's lips turned to a snarl, "Don't remind me, Talron, it was your horse that did that deed."

"Again, my prince, I am sorry."

"Sorry… it is that bitch of the waves who should be sorry… and she will be when I find her, may the gods mark that on their great scale of judgment."

"My men search for her even now, the best trackers in all of Lystbrook," Talron said.

"Liar, the best trackers are at the head of our columns… but make no mistake, I've sent my own men after her, and the reckoning will be great."

Talron's face, already haggard, lost all color.

"First Saffron, then my sister, assuming Raziel is more loyal than you, Talron."

The elder man bowed, "I serve in the best way I may."

Heat bloomed in the room and the priest fell back as the prince drew himself up on his elbows.

"You are my father's man, so I tolerate you, but make no mistake, if you get in my way during these negotiations I'll be sure you suffer a worse fate than I have planned for the shield maiden… understood?"

Talron bowed again and got to his feet, "Yes, my prince."

"Then get out, the both of you!"

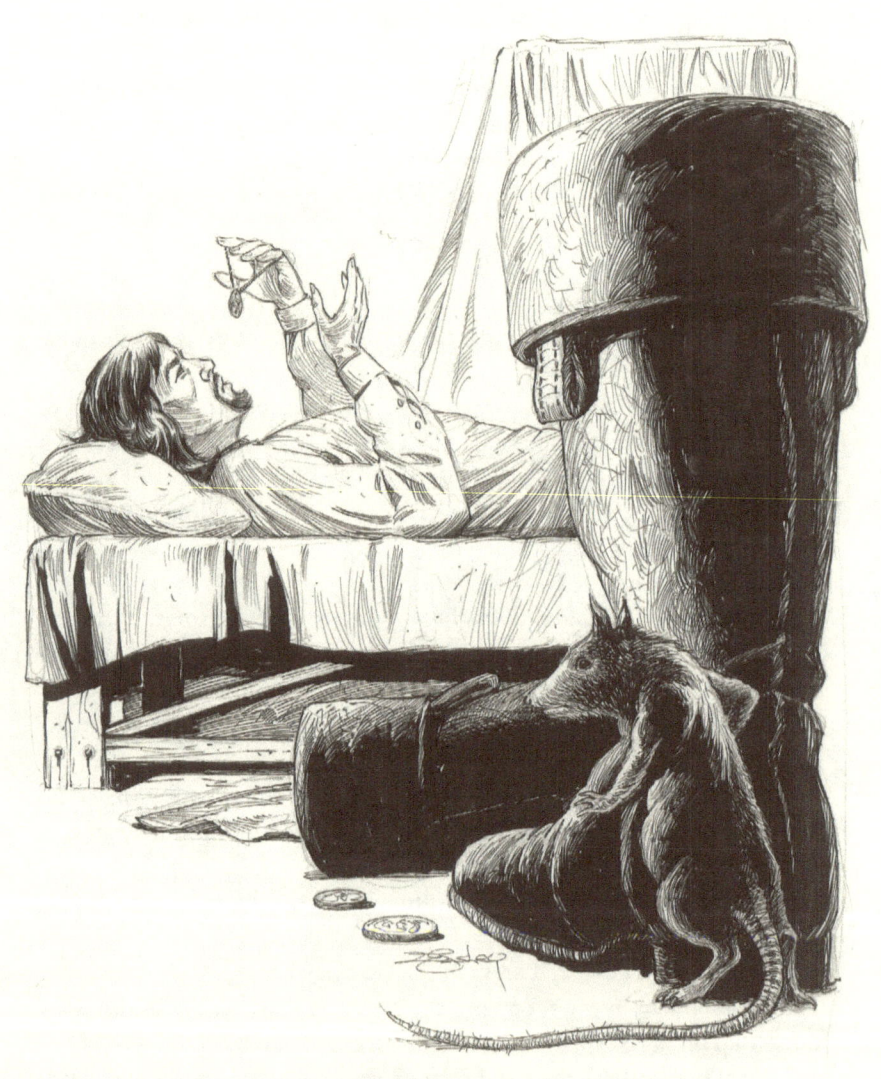

The priest and knight left the tent and the prince pulled on his britches with a wince of pain. He walked stiffly to a table, took a deep gulp of wine and then cast the cup into the corner.

"Damn these fools... when this is done I'll have to tolerate none of them..." the prince cursed.

He walked back to his bed and lay down, his hand searching beneath the folds until he withdrew a talisman that shone in the dull lamplight. It bore the likeness of a maiden bound in chains with rubies at her nipples and groin. The prince brought it to his lips and whispered a prayer.

The rat twitched. *By the Oak Father... the Hierophant was right... the dark goddess does move in the south...*

Turning from the tent, Relan raced on his little paws out of the camp. The false dawn trailed after him and by the time he finished climbing the stone rise to his camp the army below was stirring.

CHAPTER TEN

SAFFRON

*W*hy are you here? Have you stayed to watch my final destruction? Do you mock me?

Silence... always silence... Stay then, I've no other companions
now and perhaps you'll watch over my bones as they bleach in the sun
once the bounty-men have found me and done their worst.

I'm no human, no hot spark resides in my breast, and yet I find my
temper fiery more often than I care to count.

Whatever the case, I will die a woman on my own terms and not
some cow-toed whore that lives only to sate the desires of others until
I've outlived my usefulness.

This is how I am, lurking spirit, for better or worse. And make no
mistake about my loyalties, I serve the princess. I've read the knightly
scripture and taken the vows even if no man has borne witness to my
pledge.

I will move forward, I will quest, and if the blessing of the Lady
of the Deep falls to me, then I will see my Igrayn again, and she will
be protected...

The mare plodded on through the low hanging branches of skeletal
trees as Saffron made her way southeast. Five long and miserable days had
passed since the accident at Sastrine Castle and she had seen no sign of
pursuit.

Her stomach ached and her head still swam with grim thoughts of ret-ribution. She constantly saw images of her body hanging on the sea gal-lows while gulls picked her yellow eyes from her skull.

I was nothing before I was brought to Sastrine and now I've thrown it all away... Perhaps I was meant to submit, meant to bed down wth the prince and be happy with the lot I'd been gifted...

Biting her lip, she shook her head.

No... I know right from wrong, and I'd rather die than become another source for his bragging stories of conquest to his castle cohorts.

Her path led around another low tree-covered hill. The entire eastern section of the Wintertide was little more than forest covered mountains, every trail eventually leading to a dead drop of some kind.

There were no straight paths in eastern Lystbrook unless one consid-ered the smoothly navigated shipping lanes that passed the rocky shores to be straight in their course.

Her mare suddenly gave a start, and she pulled back on the reins. The beast threw its head back and forth while blowing puffs of steaming breath from its nose.

"Easy gal..." she whispered running her gloved hand over the horse's neck.

The horse calmed down but refused to go any further up the trail. Look-ing up, she focused on the old trees, most of them covered with brown-leafed vines, grown thick in patches all along the path. Up the trail, almost out of sight, a strange configuration of vines rose at an awkward angle.

Sliding from her horse, she tied the reins to a nearby tree and drew her sword with a crisp ring in the cold air. Grabbing the helm from her saddle-bag she moved up the path, slowly forcing the metal and fur-lined helmet down over her hair until the brow lip was right above her eyes.

Reaching the tangle, she inched her sword out and pushed back the dried leaves. The vines gave way enough for her to see an old pitted stone beneath. She inched forward, and with gloved hand ripped the vines off the monolith until she could see the ancient letters on the surface.

Crumbling relics, especially free-standing marker stones, could be found all over Lystbrook. They were the symbols of a lost era when druids and green Aspara ruled her nation. This particular work was similar to the sky stones she'd seen near Avonel, but as she continued to stare at it she sensed something different.

Stepping back just far enough to get a good look at the entire picture, she made out several images, but couldn't read the faded and worn words connecting them.

She saw the head of a great cat, its tongue slipping between open jaws, and facing it, the slender figure of a kingfisher. Further down the stone, a shield was depicted with a single rod pointing upward that was topped with a starburst.

The Kingfisher of the Ergoroths, the wand of the Emerald Knights of the Wintertide, but the cat means nothing to me...

She traced the feline image with her leather-clad finger until something came back to her from the teachings of Jane, the apprentice historian of the ladys-in-waiting.

The Ergoroth Queens and Kings were a noble family from the far north. Their rich blood was not what cemented their rule of Lystbrook however, it was the mighty Fleetwood line they married into which gave them the strength to rule....

She retraced the image of the cat.

The Leopard... Could this have something to do with the first Queen of Lystbrook, Sarah of the House of Fleetwood?

Looking up, her eyes wandered further down the trail and up a small hill before finally turning back to watch her horse. Her mare was waiting quietly on the path behind her, but something in its demeanor told her it would go no further.

Let me be off then, and see what mysteries await in these foreign tangles...

Saffron walked up the hill and with each turn of the path more remnants of old were revealed. At first, more of the monoliths, then fallen stone halls, and finally a path that led into the depths of a large thicket atop the crest. Each hall was little more than a stone arch descending into the earth, but all were made of heavy granite and either sealed or collapsed, denying her entry.

A burial mound, lost in the depths of the forest... but why?

From the symbols on the structures, she assumed they housed lesser knights and ladies who had served the leopard, as the cat was etched into the stones around most entries. After nearly an hour of searching the hill she stopped and wiped sweat from her brow.

I've heard the peasant tales of the Hill of Lost Bones, resting place of the First Queen, but I never believed it truly existed…

Even the ground felt dead around her. The late fall leaves and occasional wisps of snow adding to the feeling. Her boots crunched the icy ground beneath her as she continued a slow circle upward to the dome of the hill. The sun broke through the clouds enough that she could see the thicket of trees atop the mound. The cluster of bare oaks had overgrown and inter-mingled with a structure seemingly as ancient and dead as the early winter hill that surrounded it.

When she at last reached the summit, she found the remnants of a stone road that had at one time descended down the hill from the small structure on top. Although tangled with brown vines, this structure was better preserved than the others and stood hard against the elements.

This is the burial site of the first Ergoroth Queen… there can be no other explanation…

Unlike the other structures though, this one had not collapsed, and it was no longer sealed. The heavy stone door had been pulled outward some-how, face down, amid a pile of stone shards in the tall grass. It must have taken some doing, for the door was cracked in two, the top and bottom pieces no longer aligned. Adjusting her gloves and helm, she climbed over the fallen door and stepped up to the arched entryway. Although nothing barred her passage but overhanging vines, the dead leaves and brown moss gave it the same deathly aspect that emanated from the rest of the hill, and it chilled her to the bone. After a moment's hesitation, she gave her sword a mighty swing, cutting a clear path to the dim interior.

She stood at the threshold of a hall whose walls were covered with etch-ings and contained six sealed doors. Near the middle of the long crypt, she saw a stone alter radiating a dim amber glow. Above it, the roots of a tree had broken through the crypt's roof, raining pillars of golden light into the chamber's far reaches. It was difficult to tell whether the amber glow truly emanated from the table or was just a trick of the light.

Not entering, she searched the patches of shadow around the edges of the room until her gaze returned to the stone alter in the center. She could see something lying flat on the flagstone top, surrounded by a glow that mingled with the afternoon light to create an unearthly shimmer in the gloomy interior.

What is it...a weapon or some other treasure left here by those long forgotten?

Taking a step back, she nearly tripped over the fallen door, and a frown pulled at her face. She knelt, letting her hand trail down the heavy stone surface.

Surely it must have taken great effort to remove this door, but the thieves who broke the initial seal weren't able to take the treasure laid out so willingly for them...

Sliding down to rest upon the ruined lower half of the door, she drew her legs up to her chest and let the sunlight bath her face. All her senses were screaming at her to turn back, and yet some force called out to her, begging her to enter.

What curses do you hold, ancient queen, and what hope have I of overcoming them. Igrayn, if only I had your inner strength I could do this, win this battle of will and become the heroine I so long to be...

A smile passed her lips.

My princess, if you would do this, then so must I...

CHAPTER ELEVEN

ERIK

I know, I know, this whole thing is crazy, but when I get my mind fixed on something, anything, all else just kind of falls away. Ask Shera, she'll tell you, if you can find her.

I wonder sometimes if she thinks of me. Somehow two years have slipped away since last I saw her beyond the Black Gate in that cursed city of Taux. She wouldn't have aged, the Aspara never do, but these damnable southern roads and countless petty battles have certainly taken their toll on me, even at twenty-two winters... I fooled you didn't I? You thought I was older, but my journey has been long, and started at fifteen.

Ah well, better to die young chasing a dream, or a beautiful conquest, than in some lonely and forgotten room as the passing years steal your vitality. If this is my end, then so be it, but I'll not give up so easily.

Watch now, if you will, because there's certainly high adventure afoot...

They'd been traveling in waist-deep water for near an hour, the cold, brackish liquid smelling of rot and sea salt. Telluria maintained a shining globe of light floating in the air above the waterline, the illumination giving them some solace from the claustrophobic feelings they were all experiencing in the tunnels, but even light did nothing to calm the guttering chill experienced by each of the human's and Eldaryn's elemental sparks.

"I see another light." Ash said.

The Eldaryn was pale, even if he was being carried on Braxus's shoulders, the water too much for his high fire spirit to endure for such a prolonged period of time.

Braxus grumbled and adjusted the Eldaryn's weight on his shoulders as the rest of the party came to a halt. Telluria extinguished her light and slowly their eyes all adjusted to the shadow.

"Torch," Malcolm said dumbly, his finger pointed ahead.

"That means trouble," Erik said.

Blades were drawn quietly from waterlogged sheaths.

"What could be down here that would need torches?" Igrayn asked.

"If this truly is the only access point to the palace, all manner of men and beasts might have discovered this pathway over the past thousand years," Telluria said.

"If I'd wager a copper, I'd say tide goblins. The little creatures are like rats when it comes to finding places to hide and flourish, especially with a water source," Malcolm said.

"Yeah, Tide Goblins," Tavalori began. "They like to make their homes in coastal caves, but also raid the sewers of nearby cities for food. After a thousand years, it's more than possible some strays found their way here."

Erik said, "Remember, goblins are notoriously stupid, so much so that some of the things they do have an odd way of making complete sense."

"Meaning?" Telluria asked.

"Meaning they attack in a gang, and nine times out of ten they attack the largest foe first, completely ignoring all other threats until their first target is dead. It opens their flanks to an enemy, but it also has a deadly effect on a single target," Erik said.

"He's right, so be watchful and try not to make any noise," Tavalori agreed.

The water broke around them as they moved forward, but the closer they got to the flickering light the clearer it became there was nothing guarding the entrance.

"Bandylegs is with us." Ash whispered.

Todmann gave the little Eldaryn a humorous grin, but made no reply. From the underground chamber a grouping of well-worn steps led out of the water and into a single arched stone passage illuminated by two guttering torches.

"Well, I'll give the little creatures credit. They keep a well-lit lair," Malcolm said.

Erik moved up the steps, water leaking from his pants and boots as he climbed. Tavalori was close at his back, the ranger's bow nocked and ready.

The passage was built of cut stone and a light coating of lichen spider-webbed up the cracks like outstretched and misshapen fingers. Their boots sounded lightly against the stone, each turn bringing more torches and some side passages that led to refuse-strewn rooms.

"This is creepy..." Erik whispered.

Tavalori nodded and pushed past Erik, his body creeping slowly forward. He occasionally knelt down and checked the path they followed, his eyes going from the floor to the passage and then back.

"Any luck?" Erik asked.

"Bare feet have worn the stones here smooth in constant passing; they've also left a residue of dried salt along the trail," Tavalori answered.

"Then they've been going in and out of the sewers."

"So it would seem, and on a fairly regular basis," Tavalori said.

Erik held up his hand for the company to wait and then asked, "How many?"

"Impossible to tell, but I do know they've been here a long while. It takes decades of constant passage to wear stone like this."

Tavalori pointed at a smooth rut that dipped the passage directly in the middle.

"Sssssssss," a little voice hissed from further down the passage.

Looking up, Erik saw a bone thin creature no taller than Ash with bat-like ears, mottled green and blue skin, and yellow reptilian eyes staring at them from the door of an unexplored room.

Its eyes narrowed, and it turned to run, but Tavalori already had it in his sights. With a quick release of his string, a red-fletched shaft sank deep into the goblin's back and dropped it without a sound.

"Nice shot," Erik whispered.

The company moved forward, Tavalori scouting the room the goblin exited before coming back shaking his head. "Nothing, I think he may have been sleeping."

Erik leaned down and inspected the creature: its hands were black and the scales pock-marked.

"Well, we've seen no other sign of them so I have a feeling they don't live this deep under the castle. Their lair has to be higher up, and this goblin's hands are burnt, so I'd say he was a passage keeper, the torch lighter, and perhaps what would pass among their society as a guard," Erik said.

Braxus shoved the tiny corpse back into the room it had come out of. Another moment passed, the company collecting their wits before they moved on.

"Whatever the case, be ready, I seriously doubt tide goblins are the only things that have found a home in these ancient tunnels," Erik said.

The party moved on. A half dozen more twists and turns in the dungeon labyrinth and they found a stair leading up. The worn trail was a perfect guide to exiting the cellar, but both the path and the torches stopped once they made it to the top of the stair.

From further inside the palace the red glow that shown down around the exterior gave a misty report of light on the upper level.

"Ok, we've gone up, but remember absolutely no direct contact with that light," Erik said.

"May Bandylegs be with us," Ash whispered.

Their path led the company through towering archways, marble-tiled reception halls, trophy rooms, and luxurious guest suites, but nowhere had they found more evidence of goblins, or even the fabled garrison. Each window they passed was framed in iron and paneled with stained glass that diffused the light drifting into the interior. Tavalori tested the glow by releasing a captured rat into it, but the animal passed through the glow without trouble. Whatever dire magic infused the light outside the palace, the interior was safe, at least where the windows were stained.

"I've seen the palace many times from the upper towers of the Sun Temple, studied its history and construction, and from what I can tell of our journey thus far we've entered the gate pavilion," Todmann said.

"Meaning?" Erik asked.

"The royal apartments will be just beyond, and I believe the throne room lies at the very heart of the palace."

Erik turned to the others. Everyone was wet, cold, and weary.

I've got to lead here, and being on this razor's edge of nerves too long will cost us...

"Understood, let's look for a place among these outer apartments where we might rest and dry out."

The company nodded, and Tavalori took the lead again. The hall extended further back into the structure, but a massive set of wooden double doors rested in an arch to their right, and Erik called a halt.

"We'll try this one, and see what we come up with."

Malcolm and Braxus came forward and pressed their shoulders to the doors. They gave without complaint and Erik stuck his head beyond the portal.

Inside, the room was a two-story library, the heavy smell of dust and old leather wafting into the hall. Three towering stained-glass windows shed dim red light into the massive room, and from somewhere in the scarlet shadow on the second level he saw movement and heard the flapping of wings as darting black shapes flew from corner to corner.

Tavalori pushed past him, his bow down and his eyes looking up.

"Birds… how could they have gotten in here?" the woodsman asked.

"Are you sure they're birds?" Erik asked.

Tavalori nodded, "Yes, more than likely they're sparrows that were caught inside the palace somehow, or perhaps there's an opening above."

Bringing his hand to his lips, he cupped them and let out a high chirp. Erik watched the birds but they didn't respond. Tavalori took another couple of steps into the room and repeated the sounds, this time drawing an instant and lightning-fast reaction.

Like stones shot from a sling, four dark bird-like shapes fell at the youth and plunged their needle-nosed beaks deep into his flesh. The action was so sudden Tavalori didn't even have time to stagger backward, his eyes blinking in disbelief as his knees buckled and he came to rest sitting upright on the floor.

Behind Erik, Igrayn screamed and Malcolm cursed. More creatures circled down from above as Erik raised *Fury* and leapt to the defense of his fallen comrade. Incantations of *afterglow* rang out from Telluria's lips and a series of blazing bursts of energy shot towards the descending birds, dropping them from the air. Their scorched and smoking corpses had barely hit the ground before more of the creatures appeared.

Meanwhile Tavalori lolled back, eyes glazed over as the little needle-nosed birds pulsed at his neck and shoulders, their abdomens swelling with crimson fluid like a feeding mosquito. Erik swung *Fury*, the blade rending one of the birds distended sacks, spraying blood in all directions.

Ash stepped forward and flung a fine crystal powder into the air, his words calling upon Bandylegs for protection. The powder burst into action, sparks flying everywhere and lit the room with a flash great enough to confuse the flight of the little descending blood suckers. Those circling sped away up to the second level.

Malcolm swung his sword wildly through the air: green fluid splashed everywhere when it finally made contact with one of the winged creatures.

Todmann held his ground, touching the sun-symbol at his throat and whispering a prayer. Above the priest a disembodied lance of white light appeared, the tip piercing another creature before it dove through the line of Ash's floating embers of incandescent energy.

Erik struck the body of another flyer sucking on Tavalori, blood spurting up his blade and all over the floor. The smell of copper reached the heights and more flyers descended in a chirping maelstrom.

"They smell the blood!" Erik yelled.

Igrayn caught one with her rapier, but another managed to get through the whirling blades and planted its long proboscis through the chain links of Malcolm's armored back. The impact shook his defense and another flyer dove into his left arm, its needle nose sinking in all the way to its bulging eyes.

Erik removed another of the creatures feeding on Tavalori with a quick strike and grabbed him by the belt with his off hand.

"We've got to get out of here, Telluria, keep them off me!" he yelled.

Beside her, Ash squealed, another sucker chasing him under a reading table, but Todmann's spear of sunlight vaporized the creature before it could follow.

Telluria threw an arc of blue energy at a small flock that had descended from the other side of the library. With a crackling hiss, the magic crisped them all before they made it to the battle.

Braxus cut the sucker from Malcolm's back and another from his bicep, blood misting the air as both men fell back to the door.

Erik pulled Tavalori across the stone threshold, the woodsman was so pale he looked like death, eyes sunken and lips and fingers blue as an evening sky.

"Todmann!" Erik called for the priest.

Braxus splattered another winged creature and Malcolm upended a table and then wavered on his feet as he held the flank: his eyes on the upper level. Todmann moved to Tavalori, and slid to his knees beside the young man.

Above the sound of combat Todmann called to his god, his hand glowing as he placed it to Tavalori's chest.

The woodsman took a shuddering breath, his eyes fluttering open. Igrayn fell back and gave a strangled cry of relief as she saw Tavalori breathe. Erik nodded at the priest as Malcolm knocked a hungry flyer from its flight toward the door. Todmann and Igrayn helped Tavalori to his feet, the three of them staggering toward the exit.

Braxus grabbed the door and called after Ash, "We're leaving!"

The Eldaryn screamed and fled the protection of the table, his hands over his head and heat pressing the entire room as he ran. Two creatures sped at him but both narrowly missed the mark, Ash diving through the door just as Malcolm and Braxus pulled both panels closed.

The company sat in the hall, their breath coming in great gasps: the sound of chirping and impacts coming from the far side of the doors.

"Definitely not sparrows…" Erik said.

No one laughed.

After a minute Igrayn spoke, "We need to find a place for Tavalori to rest, he can't even stand."

Todmann's hands shook, and Telluria was almost as pale as Tavalori who lay shivering in Igrayn's embrace.

"I'll see what I can find," Erik said.

He got to his feet and Braxus joined him, saying, "I can't sit still after that."

Erik nodded, both of them moving further up the hall to a convergence of passages.

CHAPTER TWELVE

ERIK

*S*till here? Yes, it's all very interesting until blood starts flowing from your friends, or worse yet, yourself... What? I guess I did say friends, but don't hold that against me. I mean, this is surely a motley crew if I've ever encountered one and the only two among them I trust with half a stitch are profit hungry and self-serving mercenaries like Braxus and Malcolm.

Sure, neither one is a shining example of virtue or the knightly way, but when you meet men who you can count on to watch your back during a melee, it makes their other less polished virtues seem unimportant.

Igrayn and her young lover are another story. That fool nearly got us all killed with his stupid bird call, and Igrayn is fawning over him even more now that he's been injured. I swear, it really turns my gut to see it, and I really, I mean really, don't know why... I think I wouldn't mind so much if it was Malcolm of even Braxus, but there's just something off about Tavalori and I can't put my finger on it.

Stop it, I can almost feel what you must be thinking and I don't need a goddess trying to tell me how to run my affairs. This place we've stepped into is a death's maw, so I need to concentrate on getting out, and not on a damnable princess who only has eyes for a fool...

"Baths?" Igrayn asked.

Erik nodded and helped Tavalori to his feet, "Yep, it's a kind of octagonal bath-house and wonder of wonders, it's still working."

"Then its magic," Telluria said.

"Whatever the case, there are five connected rooms and only one easily defensible entrance. We can clean our wounds, rest, and recover there."

Igrayn helped Tavalori stand and carried his bow in one of her hands. Erik led the way, Braxus taking up a place at the rear as they slunk down half a dozen corridors and open rooms, many of them filled with oddly positioned statues.

Do I tell them the statues are probably cursed patrons of the court or simply let them dwell among their own thoughts until we've found rest...

As they reached a tiled door, Erik called a halt and checked the chamber a second time before waving them inside.

The initial room had six walls and three doors, including the exit to the main hall. It was sparsely decorated but displayed beautiful mosaics that depicted various nature scenes involving water.

"It's beautiful," Telluria said.

"If you like water..." Braxus mumbled.

They made their way inside and closed the hall door, Erik and Braxus pulling a stone bench to the door to block it.

"Braxus and I will take first watch. Malcolm, you Tavalori and Todmann can move to the bath, get cleaned up, and bandage your wounds," Erik said.

Tavalori, still shaken, didn't argue as Malcolm pulled him toward one of the interior doors. Ash walked with them to the entrance and then stood at the threshold.

"That's a lot of water..." the Eldaryn said.

"Enough for our purposes," Erik replied.

Ash turned to the other door, "What's in there?"

"Some tables and benches, and the room behind it that also connects to the baths, is filled with towels, robes, and various garments," Erik answered.

"How's that possible?" Igrayn asked.

"There must be some kind of residual preservative magic in the curse, the same thing that put the legion into their endless slumber. Instead of things growing old, it's as if the magic is bending time, keeping this place in the moment," Telluria said.

"If that's true, then things living in here might also be subject to the spell?" Erik asked.

Telluria thought a moment and then said, "I suppose."

"What are you thinking?" Braxus asked.

Thousand year-old goblins… now that's scary…

Erik scratched the back of his neck, "Things better left unsaid. Anyway, Ash, you and the ladies should get some sleep. Bed down in the room next door and leave the door open. Braxus and I will keep watch until the others are out of the baths and then we'll wake you up."

"Wake me not, I'm not taking a bath in this life," Ash said.

Erik nodded, and the trio moved into the adjoining room. Braxus sat on the stone bench, placed his head against the door and closed his eyes, saying, "Wake me if you see anything."

Erik sighed and got up to stretch his legs.

If we survive this it will be a minor miracle…

Erik listened from the shadows of the door, his position concealed enough he could barely glimpse the bathing ladies.

"The water feels wonderful…" Igrayn said.

Beside her amid the rising mist of the baths Telluria reclined with eyes closed.

"Indeed," the Wizard said.

"I wish I could enjoy it under different circumstances," Igrayn said.

"Well, I only had the muddy pools of the fens to bathe in for a century, so this is a dream no matter what the circumstance."

"I could bathe every day in the sea at my mother's palace in Avonel, and she would often say I must be descended from water instead of fire," Igrayn said.

"One of your ancestors, Sarah I believe, had Corsair blood, so she was of the elemental water," Telluria offered.

Igrayn turned to look at the woman, her face pale blue and ageless in the steam, "You've studied the history of Lystbrook?"

"I've been apprenticed for a century, Igrayn, I've studied almost all history, especially that of the old kingdoms."

"What about the current political landscape in these nations?" Igrayn asked.

"My mistress used to scry from the top of her tower, her mind taking in the affairs of many of our neighbors. She was also responsible for most contracts that passed between nations as a representative of the Order."

"Then what do you know of me?" the princess asked.

"Only that you are to be given over to marry the Ny Winter King upon your eighteenth name-day as an offering of alliance from Lystbrook to Aflyr. I can only assume you're here now to either explore the land you'll become queen of or to find what freedom you can in your final year before you become truly imprisoned by privilege."

There was silence for a long time, water dripping from bronze spigots and the sound of snoring coming from the adjacent room.

Finally, Igrayn said, "It was a gift from my mother..."

Telluria opened her eyes, "What?"

"This year, it was a gift from my mother. She well remembered going to my father in an arranged marriage and all the dreams she had as a girl being dashed on her wedding day. She didn't want that for me so she bartered a year of freedom for me, and so I came south to stay with my aunt in the guise of a minstrel."

"That seems both foolish and dangerous," Telluria said.

Heat rippled across the water, Igrayn rising from the pool and grabbing a towel. "My mother is a very wise woman, and I owe her everything for taking this chance with me."

Telluria watched the princess, the young woman dabbing the water from her skin before reaching into the linen cabinet and drawing out a sheer set of night clothes.

"Those aren't very practical for combat," Telluria said.

Igrayn turned on her, lips pressed into a thin line and brow furrowed.

"I'll not waste this year, and tonight I'll make Tavalori mine just to know that I've tasted something more than what my husband will provide!"

Igrayn pulled on the sheer undergarments, the fabric barely covering her slender curves.

"I'd say you'll live to regret decisions made in the heat of the moment, but I am not sure that any of us will live anyway," Telluria said.

"What would you know of heat?"

The words had barely slipped from Igrayn's lips when a dark shadow beside the cabinet shifted, exposing a huge claw. Telluria sat up, water cascading from her neck and shoulders, but the claw had snatched Igrayn and pulled her into the darkness before she could utter a word.

Igrayn screamed, and Telluria summoned a globe of light. At the far side of the chamber Erik burst through the doorway, sword in hand.

"There!" Telluria pointed, "Something came out of the wall and grabbed her!"

He dashed around the pool, his boots slipping on the wet granite until he was beside the cabinet. Telluria's globe rose up beside him and illuminated an indentation in the wall. Erik leaned into it, the stone sliding silently back on smooth gears and he felt the steamy heat of the room behind him being sucked past into the cavity.

"What did it look like?" he asked.

Telluria shook her head, "I don't know. Something reptilian I think."

Braxus, blinking sleep from his eyes, stumbled to the chamber door as Erik leaned into the hidden chamber, his head turning upward. "It's no more than a round vertical shaft and the thing must have had wings because it only goes up and there's no stair."

"What happened?" Braxus asked.

Erik leaned back into the room, "I've got to get up there."

Telluria nodded, her eyes closing and her hands touching at the palms. Steam rose off her naked body, the cool air turning her skin to gooseflesh. *Afterglow* flowed free, a disc of light appearing in the hollow beneath Erik's feet.

"Erik…" Braxus said.

Telluria pushed her palm upward, the disc carrying Erik out of sight.

"Gods! Where have you sent him?" Braxus's voice echoed from below.

"Up," Telluria replied.

Erik looked up, the night sky twinkling with stars as the disc propelled him toward the roof line.

By the gods I'll be shot right into the glow…

"Telluria!" he yelled.

There was no reply; the disc moving too fast and the distance between them already too great. Ducking low, he tensed as the disc burst into the sky, but the night air was crisp and clear, no sting of the crimson glow touching his features. He turned, the disc floating in space, snow-capped mountains rising in the distance as the upward motion slowed to a halt.

"Where did she go?" he whispered.

Wind whipped at his face, and he tested the disc's edge, the circle of light holding firm in the air. Below, the palace glowed, but several towers rose through the cursed light, openings in the roofs creating a vertical entrance for anything with the ability to fly.

His eyes searched the other towers. The largest, a great ruby-slated bulb of a thing lay away and below, an open window supporting the frame of a serpentine winged beast.

The creature's back was laced with muscle, rippling beneath heavy brown wings and he could hear Igrayn cursing and struggling from behind its bulk.

Standing, he marked the distance, his hand sheathing *Fury* as he pulled the loop in his belt another notch.

Perhaps thirty feet and a vertical slope of twenty…

He turned around and walked four feet back to the end of the disc.

It's not enough room…

Closing his eyes, he took a deep breath, his mind wandering back to his time in the Planer Archipelago when his master first took him on as an apprentice. He could almost see her before him, the words of her instruction echoing in his mind.

Erik touched down, his feet sending up sand before he tumbled onto his back. Shera was there, her staff smacking his shins with an impact that sent golden gulls flying into the smoke of the nether sea.

"Ouch!" *he yelled.*

"You'll get much worse when you tumble off the edge of a building," *she said.*

Nine globes, each flaming a different color of the rainbow, lit the jasmine-scented sky, each hanging like dark cataracts in the air around his master as she stood over him. She was lithe, light-chocolate skinned, with deep honey-colored hair and eyes as clear blue as polished sapphire.

Today, however, those eyes resembled storm clouds, the wind picking up around her as sand blew into Erik's eyes.

He shielded his face, his left hand running over his bruised shins as he got to his feet.

"Highborn gentlemen aren't thieves," he said.

Shera cracked him again, this time across the shoulders. He cursed and spun away, Shera saying, "They are the worst thieves of them all, especially those not likely to inherit. They spend their lives stealing from everyone around them in an attempt to maintain a lifestyle they've grown accustomed to while at their father's knee."

He frowned, "You sound like Master Arvendor…"

Shera walked to the misty shoreline her staff playing against the wisps of smoke arising from the sea.

"Arvendor was your father's man, his agent in the streets, but did you know he was a rogue before he carried the sword of a knight?"

Erik shrugged, "I'd heard as much."

"And your father gave the responsibility of training you to Arvendor. Does that seem at all suspicious?"

"I was to be given over to the ranger's hall as an emissary to the wood, what does it matter who trained me until I was cast into the forests like the trash from a noble's picnic?"

Shera turned, "Perhaps, but whatever the case, you've been a rogue's apprentice since you could walk, so my tutelage is no different."

They stared at each other, the light playing with shadows around them. Finally, Shera motioned back to their starting point further up the sand.

"Give me another jump, but this time, use your fire."

"What?"

"You know the mechanics, the hard legs, the angle for launch, the stride, the arm throw after launch, all of it, but you're not using your fire."

"My fire is here," he said pointing at his chest, "not in my legs."

Shera shook her head, "Who can jump farther, an Aspara or a Human?"

"Aspara," Erik answered.

"Why?"

"Because you have the wind around you, it's your element and it carries you."

She nodded, "True, but our energy is cold, diffuse, and hard to control. Humans, however, have fire, and fire is the most powerful energy source there is."

"But fire can't carry you through the air."

"No, but it can fuel your muscles to do things otherwise unheard of."

Erik thought on this, a grunt escaping his lips as he walked back along the beach to the starting point.

Erik pulled off his boots, Igrayn's screams turning his insides to molten lead as the wind washed over him sending steam rising from his neck and shoulders.

Wind at my back... that's good, and a downward fall should extend my range...

He pressed up on his toes then back again waving his arms and shaking out his muscles. Another scream and the sound of chains rattling stirred his soul. He caught fire, eyes focused on the nothingness before him. Heat rose from him in a palpable wave, and he closed his eyes.

One... two... three!

Pushing off, he took two long strides and then leapt into the open air. The muscles in his legs burned, his spark igniting the spring at the moment of launch. He flew through the air, wind whipping around him until he opened his eyes and looked down to see the crimson palace beneath. There were countless towers, jagged walls, and heavy stone all reaching up to claim him, to crush him against their unforgiving strength, that is, if he somehow survived falling through the glowing red light of the curse.

Gods...don't let me fall that far...

He kept moving forward, the slate shingles of the tower rising up at speed obscuring all else.

Keep your balance forward...

Head leaning in, he crashed hard into the angled slate, the tower shuddering under the impact as chips of stone shot into the air. He turned, reached, fingers scrambling for a hold as he slid down the incline.

His naked feet caught hold of something, his hands finding grips on the metal pins that held the shingles in place. Looking back, he was no more than a foot from the lip, gargoyles mocking him with their twisted faces at intervals around the circumference.

Igrayn screamed again and he adjusted his position, body leaning down over the lip as a huge shape leapt into the open sky beneath him. Without pause he grabbed a gargoyle and swung down, the open window below swallowing him up like the maw of a moaning golem.

He rolled to a stop, coming up just as the silvery moonlight was obscured in the window by the silhouette of the beast, returning nearly as quickly as it had gone.

"Kill him!"

Erik saw the speaker, a wretch of a man in red robes trimmed with gold. He wore his oiled black hair in a topknot, his bulbous forehead exposed while a thin black mustache hung limply from his yellowed upper lip. He stood above a circular stone altar, thick with candles burning down around it as he wrestled with Igrayn, trying to secure her bindings.

Looking away, Erik watched the beast drop into the room, its wings curling back behind it and its heavy musk bringing bile to Erik's throat. With the ring of steel on steel, he withdrew *Fury* from his scabbard, the demon paying the sound no mind as it swung a thick arm at his head.

He ducked, fell back and dodged a second blow that cracked a black marble tablet on the wall where etchings of dragons twisted and spat. Crouching below the thing's arms, he swung *Fury* in a horizontal arch and stuck the creature mid-thigh.

Sparks flew and two runes along the length of *Fury's* blade blazed with orange light. He sprang backward, the demon pounding at the air where he'd just crouched. He danced along the curve of the wall, but his maneuvering space was dwindling with every step back.

The robed man was cursing, spittle flying from thin lips as he secured the final shackle. Igrayn struggled atop a circular slab, old blood flaking off from beneath her back and a dozen thick candles burning around her.

"Igrayn!" he called.

She turned toward him and he took a step toward the altar but the beast was suddenly there. Its meaty fist slammed into his shoulder and sent him tumbling against a wall. He heard bone snap, his left arm dangling as stars swam in his vision.

Two great steps and the demon was on him again, putrid breath against his cheek as it extended dark claws toward his throat.

Asgard's promise… be true as ever…

"Raseri …" he whispered with the last of his hope as he clutched the hilt of his sword.

From his right hand healing magic spread up and through his shoulder, light casting cruel shadows up the demon's chest and over its grotesque face. He felt time slow, snowflakes outside the window stopping mid-fall and the light of the candles flickering like shuddered lamps thrown closed and then open again. The beast stood near frozen as well, the approach of its claws stopping just short of crushing his throat.

Fury blazed to life, the fire-forges of Yggdrasil, the world tree, lighting up three more war runes upon the wide blade. Erik thrust the sword up, the tip penetrating the demon's breast with a blaze of blue sparks.

A hiss split the night, screams filling the tower as the demon's fingers fell away from Erik's neck, black blood rushing down the blade. Each drop of blood trembled, reached, and spat hissing curses as it fell to the stone floor, the demon stumbling back with a final roar before exploding in a shower of screeching souls.

The robed mage wailed, the shades turning back on him, creating a cloak of darkness. Golden florescence surged up to defend him, a swirling maelstrom of light and dark enveloping him as he fell away from the altar.

Erik stumbled to his feet, *Fury* blazing in his hand and time still drifting by in a haze of slowed movement. The blades full power was in bloom, healing energy knitting the bones in his shoulder and speed enchantments quickening his every move. He rushed to Igrayn, her eyes wide and mouth holding a scream that was frozen on her tongue.

He brought *Fury* down on the chains, the enchanted blade breaking them asunder with a squeal of futile protest.

Pulling her free, he dropped beneath the altar and held her to his chest, the sounds of the mage's death-throws echoing about the chamber as time refastened in his body. He wrapped both his arms around her, heat from her fear washing over him as darkness flowered in the room, a last terrible scream breaking against the black walls before all went quiet.

Then there was nothing but their breathing and the wind playing against the frame of the open window.

"Erik..." she whispered.

He pressed his stubble-covered chin against her hair, eyes closed and fingers stroking her naked back.

"Yes."

"Why?" she asked.

"Why what?"

"Why did you come for me?"

She pulled away and looked up at him, her eyes like shards of amber. His spark flared, the heat from them both rising in palpable wisps against the chill of the night.

"I'd never saved a princess before, so I couldn't let the chance slip by," he smiled.

She stared at him a moment longer, then fell back against his chest.

"Pity," she said.

"I'm sorry?" he asked.

"I said pity. I just thought there might have been another reason you risked your life to save me."

Erik leaned his head back against the stone, the smell of candles heavy above his head.

Perhaps... but nothing worth having isn't worth the wait... or so Shera used to tell me...

Erik's feet were numb, and Igrayn shivered beside him as she tried to hold the candle while shielding it. She was wearing his undershirt, and he only his breeches as both of them were without shoes and his bare chest was covered in gooseflesh.

"How much farther?" she asked.

"I don't know. The stair curves so I can't count the levels and even if I could I'm not sure how high we were to begin with."

She drew closer to him, the candle flickering and their shadows dancing on the walls. *Fury*, tip out, led the way, each step circling down until they finally reached a thick wood door. Erik disengaged from Igrayn and pressed his palm against the frame, his fingers trailing down until he found a crossbar held in place by two sturdy rings of iron.

"Take my sword," he said.

Igrayn took it, a small grunt escaping her lips before he helped her balance it on her shoulder.

"Give me some light."

She slid the candle forward. Erik swung both hands up under the bar. It gave with a pop and he slid it out of the rings and placed it against the frame.

"Stay quiet, we don't know what's outside the door."

Taking back his blade, he pulled on an iron grip and the door swung inward. The hall beyond led straight away, no other doors showing along its length although three stained glass windows illuminated the passage with a soft red glow.

"It's clear," he said.

"Have you seen it before, do you know where we are?" she asked.

"No."

She grabbed his arm before he could venture out of the door. "Erik..."

He turned, "Yeah?"

"Since there's a good chance we won't make it out of this alive, I want to say thank you now," she said.

"We're not going to die here, I promise you that."

He watched her looking at him, her eyes flickering with a warm amber glow even as she shivered. Her lips, always adorable, were swollen and red, as were her cheeks and he smiled like a child before her puzzled gaze.

"You're serious, aren't you?" she asked.

"Yes."

"What do you know?"

He turned back to the hall and shook his head, "A man of my trade never divulges his secrets for free and you already owe me."

She stifled a laugh, but when he reached back his hand she took it, the two of them moving up the hall. It was warmer here, but they stayed close, their sparks flicking spasmodic heat into their bodies as Erik led them down hall after hall until he finally stopped.

"What?" she asked.

"I've been here before."

She looked in either direction but he pulled her along before she could say anything, the two of them coming to a large door set in a stone frame etched with dancing nymphs.

"The baths!" she said.

He nodded, his fist pounding the door.

"Malcolm, Braxus, it's me, open up!" he shouted.

His voice trailed dangerously down the hall, but no threat materialized as the echo of the stone bench being drawn away sounded through the door.

Malcolm opened the door, eyes wide and sword at the ready. Braxus stood beside him, the remainder of the party a few feet back, all ready for battle.

"By the gods..." Braxus said.

"Yeah, I know, now get us some clothes and I'll try to explain..." Erik said.

He pushed Igrayn into the room and closed the door, then slid the stone bench back into place.

CHAPTER THIRTEEN

RELAN

I pray to thee as I watch these men… What looms in a future where a man of the wood, a druid, holds sway over so many foreign lives? I've followed your teachings, apprenticed to your greatest disciple, but I've never been faced with such a weighty task.

I know the tales of the Strangler's Deep, the sacrifice of the God Spires, but am I capable of such an act?

Your thoughts press upon me, your mind shadowed yet present as I wait among your blessed trees, and yes, I can only accept that you are the Oak Father for it gives me some solace and comfort.

Why have you come? Is this a test? What resolve do I take on this road to ruin? Am I protecting your venerable wood or am I tipping a scale that should stay within the balanced plane of nature's neutrality?

This is my lot, then, to be the ultimate judge of what is to be in the Wintertide… I came here to find a young man and yet you divert my quest with greater things… always watching in silence.

I will do your bidding, I will be the winter to these men's lives, but know that once such power is released, your humble servant will be forever changed… but again, that might be what you have sought in the first place…

Below, just as the first trickling rays of light bled out of the eastern sky with golden fingers, the sound of falling trees marched up the hills from the glen.

Three days… three days of talks between the two sides to settle this without bloodshed and now it's come to this…

Relan walked along the heights, trees snapping at the sharp bite of axes and the pull of ropes. The Citadel of the Moon, emerald and ancient, stood in a ring of movement, the invading army like ants circling a fallen wasp.

Stopping below a pine, Relan leaned against his staff, the trio of firebirds shining, and sighed.

I listened to each parlay, in the guise of a sparrow amid the tangle of men, and yet I still have no idea what the final argument concerned. The Knights of the citadel held firm in their belief that nothing wrong was done in the name of the King and yet his son grew increasingly belligerent and furious…

The struggle for power is at hand amid this plot, the touch of the dark goddess, and I see her power rotting the very foundation of the old kingdom of Lystbrook…

Raising his staff, he closed his eyes and called on his elements, fire and air, the winds blowing around him in a warm cascade.

A wife and a hearth fire… these are the things I long for… not so many deaths on my hands…

Waving his hand before him, he drew symbols in the air, wisps of steam trailing his fingers.

> "As the seasons pass,
> cold will blanket the land
> like the thick fur of the creatures
> who must endure it…"

Around him the temperature dropped, and mist rose from his mouth. The *Phoenix Staff* surged to life, the wings of the firebirds glowing in the dawn light. Heat swept down his arm, the staff warding the frigid air away.

Again his hand passed before him, more mist-wreathed runes appeared before being struck from the air by the increasing wind.

> "As the seasons pass,
> the wind will whip over the land
> and through the land
> as the creatures take wing
> to find calmer skies and warmer climates…"

From the south a gale blew, wind tearing at his cloaks and stinging his cheeks. The wood moaned, trees swaying as the heavy clouds of winter swept over the forest in a wave.

Down in the valley at the fortress, the men looked up and cursed. They pulled down hoods and cast cloaks about them as taskmasters lashed out with heavy whips and dire words. Work continued, but the horses became wild and banners upon the fortress battlements were taken down by scrambling men, a few being ripped from their hangings by the whipping winds.

"As the seasons pass,
snow will fall,
and the earth will sleep under it,
leaving the world white as the dress of a virgin bride…"

High above, the sky turned a death-mask of grey, a flash of lightning rippling across the clouds as large white flakes began to fall.

"Oak Father, hear my calling. Bring the cleansing storm. Bathe the forest in a blanket so heavy that no beast can rise from under it and no man can tread atop it. Oak Father, bless me with thy power…"

The *Phoenix Staff* hummed, and Relan clung to it. With a swirl of icy wind, the snow picked up, white sheets coming down from the darkening clouds.

Around him the world turned white, and he clung to his staff, legs buckling as he slumped beneath the great boughs of a sheltering pine. Tremors tore through him and his eyes glazed over.

We have held this power since dragons flew the sky like birds and the Wizards were only water spirits without true magic…hold your power, master your will and the storm will continue…

Day lost its light, the storm devouring everything into a deep grey gloom. Relan rocked beneath the tree, its great green branches pressed down with snow creating a natural tent-like shelter. He lost his vision, the grey turning to black as night hid the storm behind a veil of biting wind and cold nothingness.

Cast my fire, nurse my air… feel the joined sparks of my parents and hold the world in your palm… you cannot sleep, you must stay awake…

Dawn broke with tired shadow, the pine limbs bowed to the ground. The *Phoenix Staff* lit his shelter, drips of water sliding down the shaft before the heat turned them to mist that iced among the branches above.

Relan finally sighed, shivered, and fell forward into the bed of needles around him. His hands clung to the staff, but his eyes were closed and his breath ragged. Outside the wind broke, clouds parting as sunlight pierced the cover to illuminate a world covered in white that shone like a million diamonds in a dragon's horde.

Sleep found him, dragged him down into its deep bosom as the world outside stood still, not a sound touching the air for fifty miles in any direction.

Relan awoke to silence, his breath a wisp of white smoke as he raised himself from the needles and pulled the *Phoenix Staff* close. He trembled, his eyes sunken, and his skin tight over his bones.

So much energy... a body isn't meant for such magic...

Rising, he tumbled down at once, before trying again. This time he cast much of his weight on the staff and began digging through the pine boughs that held back the snow. It took him several minutes, his breath coming in gasps and his body covered in a lather of sweat.

A brisk wind kicked snow along the heights, tails of ghostly drifts twisting like a sea serpent through the wood. A wall, twelve feet tall, of powdery snow lay in front of him and he sighed as tiny cascades of it fell into the shelter he'd used during the summoning.

I'm no good in this form, I'll need another...

Raising his hand to the sun he focused his fire, the energy of his spark mixing with the wind and firing magic through his blood.

"Tides of change blow through me, set me to wing..." he whispered.

His cloaks turned brown, the fabric shifting around his arms and torso as the magic of his druidic craft filled the air. He shrank, twisting and falling in on himself until only a sparrow remained.

Tweets broke the silence and he took to the air with the wind pushing him up around the treetops as he surveyed the glacial transformation of the valley below.

Smoke rose from the citadel and men shoveled snow along the battlements, their tabards flashing emerald in the morning light.

He circled back, tiny black eyes scanning the wasteland around the mighty keep. The snow held the signs of carnage beneath its virgin blanket, only a random lance or jutting standard with frozen banner giving sign of human habitation.

Setting atop a branch, tiny wings clearing a spot, he noted the half-built towers and siege engines like skeletal reminders of death.

I've done this… it's on me now and I must live with the consequence…

A bell tolled in one of the citadel's towers, holy chants going up into the breeze as Relan took flight again. He sailed over the keep once more, wings fighting the breeze and then turned to the southwest along the line of the falling sun.

Lystbrook brought this folly, but no king led the doomed procession… it is with him I'll have a word before this matter is laid to rest with the frozen bones of his army…

CHAPTER FOURTEEN

ERIK

You've done it now, and yes I blame you and your meddling...I want her... I saw every inch of her perfect body through that near as not there clothing she had on. Felt a good deal of it too, as I held her those minutes in the tower, but I didn't make a single rash move.

Why? How about you tell me, oh mighty goddess... Perhaps I didn't want to offend you, or perhaps you stayed my hand with a gentle and unseen reprieve, but I couldn't bring myself to do what her eyes were inviting me to do.

It's a surprise, you know, having resisted what was ripe for the picking. I feel like the past two years have bled out beneath me and once again the lessons learned alongside my master Shera among the Isles are echoing in my head. She was my steady hand, my guide when I was coming from the lofty halls of a wanton, over privileged youth. The past few years, away from her, I've lived a lie, once again shrinking from responsibility and thinking only of myself. But now I look at Igrayn and somehow I'm stayed.

I blame you and your watchful eye... you who so reminds me of Shera and her ever-present wisdom. I promise you I've never striven to be a better man, what purpose was there in it? Do better men live better lives? Not in my experience, and yet as much as I want to be gluttonous and self-satisfying I'm here doing things better left to story-book heroes...

By the all the gods in the heavens this is not me...

Erik took another step, Tavalori close at his heels. Behind, the party watched, Igrayn tucked safely in their middle with eyes furtive and dark.

She'll not recover soon enough for me… this place is a hive of dangers and while we may not require her rapier in combat, we do need her concentration…

Raising his hand, he motioned for a halt, a set of double doors blocking their path.

"Telluria, I'll need light," Erik said.

The Wizardress walked forward, hand raised as a globe of energy manifested in her palm. He watched her light drift up the frame, his hands pushing the doors open. The tang of sea-water filled the air, and although his spark fluttered at his proximity to her, he stayed close, the darkness inside the room waning.

"It is a large chamber, but something's covering the windows," Erik said

"Curtains?" Todmann asked.

Erik shook his head, the hairs on the back of his neck twitching. "Possibly, but there is an earthy odor mixed with Telluria's magic, something magical might be involved."

Todmann fingered the jade talisman at his neck and Tavalori pushed up next to Erik.

"I sense it too, something of earth, perhaps we're close to a garden."

Erik nodded, "Keep your eyes open. This is one of the last rooms in this section of the building, and we can't afford to miss anything like we did in the baths."

Telluria stayed at his back, her light making shadows flow over an immense wooden table that stretched beyond the sphere of illumination. Chairs were set along its sides, and pillars stretched upward into the darkness that partially obscured a vaulted ceiling full of architectural latticework.

The shuttered windows were covered with tangled masses of brown-leafed vines that twisted up into the dim recesses of the ceiling and snaked down across the marble floor. Here and there the vines disappeared in a spider web network of cracks in the marble floor.

The party fanned out, swords at the ready. Each shadowed figure searched around the pillars while trying to stay in the space illuminated by Telluria's light.

"What was that?" Ash asked.

The Eldaryn spun in place, his eyes darting among the rafters.

"What was what?" Braxus asked. "I didn't hear anything."

Malcolm pushed a chair from under the table with his boot and lowered his head down slowly beneath the heavy horizontal plain.

Igrayn yelped, her cry drawing the focus of the others as she raised her rapier.

"What?" Erik asked.

"Something touched me!" she said.

Braxus moved closer to her, as did Tavalori.

"The tables clear," Malcolm said from his kneeling position.

Everyone relaxed, but Igrayn screamed again as a thick leafy vine reached down from the ceiling, grabbed her and pulled her up. A second appendage struck Braxus, the blow sending him back between two pillars, his sword and throwing-axe clattering on the floor.

Igrayn stabbed the thing with her rapier, but another vine grabbed her and pulled her further into the recesses of the ceiling.

"Fire, we need fire!" Erik yelled.

Telluria fell back a step, her hands maintaining the globe, "I can't, or we lose our light."

Igrayn screamed, and an arrow flew past her, lodging in a massive jaw that appeared out of the shadows between the stonework.

"Ash!" Erik called, trying not to panic.

The Eldaryn had his pack on the floor and was furiously yanking things from it, "I'm trying!"

Erik looked up, the gaping maw utterly terrifying. It was a black void rimmed in several rows of pointed teeth, the stink of old dirt pouring down over them in a wave of corruption.

Gods... no...

It happened in an instant, the enormous mouth closed over Igrayn and she disappeared. Erik stared in disbelieving horror.

Ash brought up a black curved wand, one end an open tube and the surrounding veneer of wood covered with intricate carvings of dragons.

"Marasa!" the little man yelled.

There was a crack of thunder, smoke rising from the wand and a shower of leaves falling from the darkness above. A dark, thick, liquid splattered the top of the feasting table, some black, some crimson, and Erik pulled his eyes away, looking back to the support pillars.

"Bring it down, cut the stems!" he yelled, jerking back into action.

Malcolm moved with him, both men slashing at vines wrapped around the pillars as more rope-like appendages curled and flipped in the air above

the table. Behind them Todmann chanted a prayer, the man's jade talisman flaring to life as he pointed it to the ceiling.

Light burst forth, revealing a creature more head than body, yellow eyes rolling wildly as it shook and twisted. Telluria dropped her globe, its light lost in the lasting flare made by the priest of the Sun God.

She closed her eyes, hands balling up to amass *afterglow* between them. Above, the beast shook again, this time falling half the distance to the top of the table as some of its tentacular arms gave way. Liquid dripped from the corner of its mouth, the smell of the sea so powerful it drown out the scent of earth.

Erik looked at Telluria, but she'd opened her eyes and was staring at the creature as it struggled, finally opening its massive mouth to expel a mass of foaming seawater.

Igrayn, wet but seemingly whole, struck the table with a thud, water splashing in all directions as the creature continued to shake and roll its eyes.

Tavalori fired an arrow and then another, both shafts sinking into the creature's left eye. It fell another few feet, and Erik jumping up on the table with *Fury* raised high.

"Just a few more feet!" he called.

Malcolm began cutting the few vines that still clung to the base of the pillar.

Telluria threw her hands out, a blast of yellow energy striking a mass of supporting tendrils that roped from the beast's scalp suspending its head. The thing tipped wildly, fire bursting out along the skinny threads of its outer appendages.

The creature fell another few feet and Erik swung his sword, the tip slicing the thing's chin open and spilling more blood down upon the table. Beneath him Igrayn choked, Todmann pulling her from the table as she expelled water from her lungs in great heaves.

More arrows flew and Erik continued to hack away, the creature quaking and hissing until it let loose its hold on the ceiling and crashed to the floor. Malcolm and Erik were on it, Braxus joining them with his axe, blood streaming from a cut above his eye.

Away from the butchery, Igrayn sat rocking and whispering the same words over and over, some sort of chant or prayer.

Finally, the beast lay still, reduced to a sloppy heap of vegetable pulp and Todmann's talisman darkened and cooled, leaving the room in dim shadow once again. Erik sheathed *Fury* and walked to where Tavalori crouched protectively next to Igrayn. Todmann and Ash stood over the couple and Erik looked to the spiritual men for answers.

"Is she . . .?" Erik trailed off.

Igrayn's eyes opened, "I'm fine."

Eyes once amber-gold were now green as emeralds and when she looked at him her fire was gone. Could this be the same woman he knew?

"How?" Tavalori asked.

"I think the sea, the elemental power of water, or an ocean deity had something to do with it," Telluria said.

"Yah, think?" Erik replied. His sarcasm was cut by the dark eyes of all his fellows.

"My flame is gone, replaced by the calming flow of water," Igrayn said.

Braxus shook his head, "You can't just switch elements," then paused before adding, "can you?"

"It has happened, when some ancestor bore a different element than the one currently held by its descendent, although doing so typically aligns with the will of an elemental God," Telluria said.

"Or Goddess," Erik whispered.

"She is the Bride of the Deep," Igrayn said. "She came to me, coaxed me, offered me a deal."

That wasn't the goddess I was talking about... What games do the gods play now?

"What kind of deal," both Braxus and Ash said in unison.

Igrayn turned to look at them, a thin smile on her face, "God's aren't the sharing type, I'd have thought the two of you would know that."

The three stared at each other a long while until Tavalori broke the silence, "Let's be away from here, we've got wounded to tend to. This damnable place will not rest until we're dead or the threat is abolished."

Erik nodded, as did the rest of them, the new Igrayn taking Tavalori's arm before casting a look in his direction, a smile creeping across her lips.

Oh... you still want to play do you? Then let the game resume...

Erik was wrested from slumber by the sounds of whispering nearby. A ring of furniture stood around the party and his few minutes of stolen sleep faded into his tired body like it had never occurred.

Gods... what now? Didn't I just finish my watch?

Ash and Braxus looked to be having an animated discussion. The Eldaryn looked up and pointed to Igrayn, the princess snuggled close to the Tavalori, partially obscured by the low cushions of a divan.

What are those two up to?

Ash twitched his nose, drew a pinch of dust from his vest and tossed it in the air. The powder shimmered and disappeared in a subtle flash, Malcolm turning from his watch with a furrowed brow.

Ash waved and the warrior nodded, turning back toward the door of the chamber. Braxus whispered something to Ash, both looking back to Igrayn as Tavalori sat up and started sneezing without relent.

Igrayn quickly detached herself from him, the young man having an uncontrollable fit for a full minute, snot streaming from his nose and his eyes watering madly.

Erik held his lips firm as he got to his feet, laughter held in check as Igrayn tried to help her young paramour recover.

"This place is damn dusty, friend, you should watch where you sleep," Braxus said.

Tavalori looked angry and the rest of the party began to stir. Erik moved to stand beside Malcolm, the man sheathing his blade and stretching.

"Nothing more here, save three doors that lead to trashed cooking chambers, and a single great door that leads to what appears to be an inner solar," Malcolm said.

Erik looked back at Telluria who smiled as she helped Todmann to his feet.

"Solar?" Erik asked, "You mean some kind of glassed-in chamber?"

Malcolm nodded, "Yes, but much larger. It's a massive dome that's been covered in the same colored glass we've seen in so many rooms of this palace. Instead of a sitting room it encloses an overgrown garden filled with white roses, twisting paths, the sound of water, and all that nonsense. It even has trees growing in it!"

"Can you see beyond it?" Tavalori asked.

"Yes, it may only be a hundred to a hundred fifty feet across, yet the growth and glass gives it a much larger feel," Malcolm answered.

"Ah, it's the legendary Queen's garden, and I've seen the massive dome that encloses it from the towers of my temple. It was said to be one of the true wonders of the Old Kingdoms," Todmann said.

"What about the light in there?" Erik asked.

"Harmless, the crimson glow doesn't penetrate the dome, so I'm not sure if it's the colored glass or some other magic at work," Malcolm said.

"I'd say the latter," Todmann said.

Erik tightened his sword belt, "I see no other option. This garden must have been the throughway into the royal pavilions, at least from these buildings. When I was above, I saw no openings in the crimson field, so we'll have to believe the light is neutralized by the glass dome, the same as it is with the other windows in the palace."

The party mumbled agreement, each taking a moment to secure their meager possessions. Ash made his way to the front, drawing up to Erik and pulling at his belt.

"Do you think we're close?"

Erik looked down at him. "I really don't know, but Todmann seems to have a good lay of the grounds and judging by the look I had from above, I'd say we're getting very near the heart of the place."

Ash sneaked a look back at Todmann but held his tongue.

"Is there a problem?" Erik asked.

"No..." Ash replied slipping back behind Erik.

Erik shook his head as he walked up to Malcolm who stood at a large door.

Malcolm pointed, "See the hinges, they've been greased and well used."

"And the floor here shows heavy signs of traffic," Tavalori added.

"More Tide Goblins?" Erik asked.

Tavalori nodded, "I'd assume. There are no boot prints and the scattering of dust marks the passage of smaller creatures."

Erik drew *Fury*. "Remember what was said yesterday about goblins choosing a single target and keep a sharp eye open as a thicket can house more of the little buggers than one would think."

Gripping the handle, Erik pulled the door upon, and the sound of running water greeted the party.

The chamber was filled with plants and trees along a twisting stone path. At the center, just visible over the blooming foliage was a large stone fountain. Tangles of vines and white roses lurked among the tall grass and Erik stepped aside to allow Tavalori the lead.

The woodsman walked softly as he entered the area, his bow at the ready and his hunting knife close at hand.

After ten feet, Tavalori turned back and gave the signal to follow. The rest of them moved into the garden, the door behind quickly and ominously becoming a dark portal just out of reach. They slunk around the path and passed several low hanging trees until coming to the fountain. The old marble spout still splashed clear water into a basin below it, the sound of its gurgling fall amplified by the glass dome above.

Tavalori paused at the basin, his eyes inspecting the ground around it.

"They've been drinking here," he whispered.

Erik frowned and looked around at the thick undergrowth.

Alongside Tavalori, Igrayn let her fingers touch the splashing water, her mouth whispering a prayer to her new found goddess. The moment her fingers brushed against the surface, a series of hisses came from the garden around them. Everyone shifted position, a second chorus of rasping calls answering the first few.

"Igrayn, don't touch their water!" Erik yelled.

From every direction slithering movements sounded from among the grasses. Braxus pulled his axe and held it in his off hand, while Ash slunk inside the heart of the company and withdrew his dragon wand.

The surrounding bush exploded with little creatures.

"Watch yourselves!" Malcolm cried.

Braxus was the first to be attacked, a rush of four blue-green goblins leaping from the undergrowth at him. The little creatures fought with claws, fangs, and small metal utensils with equal vigor.

Braxus hammered the first one with a downward stroke of his sword, and a second fell dead with its skull cleaved clean in two by his axe, but the final two made it through and cast themselves against his lightly armored legs.

The first one was whacking him with a dull knife, and the second bit the mercenary's knee with its row of pointed teeth. He cursed but before he could attack again, three more goblins appeared to take the place of the two he'd killed.

Another group of creatures came from behind the fountain, their rage focused on Igrayn. Tavalori jumped between the goblins and the princess, his heavy boot sending one of the attackers sailing into a rose bush.

Malcolm leapt in to help Braxus, his blade taking the heads off several of the warrior's new attackers. Erik did the same for Tavalori, the little creatures now attacking the woodsman instead of the princess. Telluria blasted any movement she could see inside the brush with darts of sizzling *afterglow*, the magic sending death blows in all directions.

Around the group the creatures screamed in rage and the throws of death, but still more came on. Tavalori staggered, surprised, as one of the creatures managed to jump onto his back. Igrayn lanced the creature with her rapier, and it fell dead at her feet.

After less than a minute, blood was everywhere, the melee growing more chaotic and hopeless as the party's stamina faltered. Around the combat area the grass slithered and the bushes bent and swayed as though a puppet master worked their sickly green limbs.

Beside Erik, the rose bush that had been the resting place of the first goblin booted by Tavalori was now blood red at the center, with a ring of pink roses further out. The plant reached out with its thorny branches and plucked a passing goblin from the path as it charged Tavalori.

"The garden lives!" Erik cried.

Turning *Fury* from Tavalori's attackers, he cut a branch away from the hem of Todmann's robes.

"Blood roses..." Malcolm called.

In the center of the pitched battle, Ash aimed his weapon and discharged another thunderous attack. A goblin was thrown back into a bush, blood seeping from a wound in its chest.

More goblins appeared, their numbers seemingly endless, and Ash screamed, dropped his wand, and drew a vial of dark liquid from his pack. Inside the glass, the thick greasy oil swam and danced, and Erik shouted warning, "If that's bottled fire Ash, you're more fool than I thought!"

Rushing from behind Todmann and Telluria, Ash raised the vial above his head, cocked back his little arm, and let it fly toward the closest thicket.

"Bandylegs be with me..." he whispered.

His toss was true, the bottle floating in the air until he mouthed a word and it exploded above the mass of plant-life. Sticky flame leapt skyward, casting burning globs of fluid across the leaves and branches, setting it ablaze like a candle. With piercing screams, more goblins rushed away from the flames and ran about in confusion and pain, spreading fire to anything they touched.

Erik spun away from a flaming goblin, the creature slamming into a nearby blood rosebush, setting it alight.

Amid the chaos, the garden hissed and swayed as though trying to move away from the consuming inferno.

Above them, glass shattered, and a square column of crimson light shown like a pillar of death amid the foliage. More screams filled the chamber, the red light blackening a patch of greenery in seconds.

As the vegetation next to the combat withered to nothing, more than half a hundred goblin bodies became visible. While some unfortunate creatures were burned, cloven with blade or sucked dry by the dangerous plants, there were others that had fallen victim to the cursed light.

Malcolm helped Braxus to his feet, the mercenary having fallen to his knees on heavily wounded legs from the repeated goblin assaults. Tavalori was in little better shape, yet Igrayn still fought on beside him, her swing taking the head from a rogue straggler that was stabbing at the woodsman with the sharpened handle end of a serving spoon.

"We've got to get out of here. The fire is spreading," Malcolm called, pulling Braxus further along the now clear path to the northwest.

Erik helped Tavalori stand, and Igrayn supported him. Beside him Telluria joined her thumbs together and sent a curved blast of energy of into the surrounding plants at their rear, the newly lit brush screeching and shaking in the wake of a painful *afterglow* kiss.

"We'd better find what we're looking for, because the exit behind us has been closed by fire," she said.

Erik nodded and covered her retreat, the party moving after Malcolm as he pressed his way toward another large door. Behind them, more windows shattered, spraying bits of glass, and providing fresh air to fuel the blaze. The vaulted dome was rapidly disintegrating, destroying their only protection from the cursed light above them.

When Erik reached the door he pulled the ringed handle but it didn't give.

"Locked," he said.

"Pry bar…" Braxus whispered.

Erik moved back and drew an iron bar from a leather strap on Braxus's pack. Rushing back to the door he slid the bar between the aged wooden panels and then moved it up until it caught.

"Hammer!" Erik yelled.

Malcolm released Braxus to Todmann's care and drew a small hammer from his own pack, handing it over. Erik took it and held the bar with his right hand before swinging the hammer upward into the underside of the bar. The stroke's impact lifted the bar a bit before it came back down again.

"Malcolm, give me a hand here. When I strike the underside of this bar and it moves up, I want you to keep it raised. Don't let it fall after any strike," Erik instructed.

The warrior nodded taking the bar in both hands, and again the hammer rang against the metal.

"I think you should hurry," Telluria commented after looking behind her.

Erik looked back. The room was filling with smoke and several taller trees were now on fire. He turned back and brought the hammer up with two hands. The stroke sung into the chamber and was drowned out by the cracking of flames, but the impact was enough.

On the other side of the door there was a loud thump. Malcolm helped force the bar upward until it finally gave and slipped free of the gap between the panels.

Malcolm pulled inward and the double doors gave. Quickly, the party entered another area of the palace, slammed the doors behind them, and took a collective breath.

"His body will recover," Todmann said.

The priest's hands glowed slightly as he waved them over the tattered knees of Braxus. Beside him, Tavalori rested: bandages harvested from the priest's pack were already wrapped around his legs and abdomen.

Erik shook his head and looked back to the door. Less than a dozen minutes after they'd fled the burning chamber, the entire glass dome had given way, and all sounds of the pandemonium within had stopped in an instant.

Whatever had happened in there, the likelihood of our exiting the palace using that room collapsed with the roof...

"How long?" Erik asked.

"An hour until he walks, two until he could fight," Todmann answered.

Malcolm was close by, eyeing a massive gilded doorway that was the focal point of a great foyer with halls leading in two other directions. Reliefs of fabled fire serpents, gladiators, and phalanx's of bronze-armored legions decorated the surfaces leading up to the door.

"That's a long time to be exposed along an indefensible corridor..." Erik trailed off.

"The wounds were not great, but they were many, and my magic has its limitations," Todmann said.

Erik nodded and turned to the waiting door, saying, "Beyond that foyer we should find the throne room and then the royal apartments. What we've come for will be in those chambers or not here at all."

Turning back to the party, he looked at Braxus. "Braxus, I've known you for half a year and in that time I've never seen you slowed... can you walk?"

Todmann started to protest but the warrior stayed him with a hand on his shoulder.

"I've had worse and been forced to march," Braxus replied.

The warrior stood, staggered once, and then straightened his back. Igrayn stared up at him then turned to Erik, her hand holding Tavalori's.

"You can't be serious?" she said.

Telluria got to her feet, as did Ash.

Erik nodded, "I'm deadly serious. This place will be the death of us, sooner rather than later and you should be more keenly aware of that than any of us."

She shook her head, but Tavalori interrupted her, "He's right, we must go on."

CHAPTER FIFTEEN

SAFFRON

What light is this in the dark that draws me near? There are strange things about, motes of presence in my mind's eye that tell me something incomprehensible.

I sit on a precipice. I know this just as surely as I've known all my life I was different from those around me. Do you watch me to witness my decision? Or do you only wish to know firsthand the cruelty of my doom or the sweetness of my salvation?

Whatever the case, I must go forward. I must face the demons of my past and face the foes of my future, or I am nothing, just some simple girl who will fade from the memory of those who once knew her...

The feeling had left her legs long ago but still she squatted, her body like a statue in the shadow before the shattered opening of the tomb. Saffron blinked twice, settled the last of her nerves and then stood. Blood rushed from her abdomen to her head and legs at the same time, and she wobbled but steadied herself, stretching until the pins and needles left her feet.

She took a deep breath.

"Goddess of the Depths... bring me strength..."

Stepping forward, she placed her boot beyond the threshold of the hall of tombs...nothing happened. Steeled by the first step, she took another, then another, each one taking her closer to the glowing table.

When she passed the first doors, one on either side of her, the temperature began dropping and her breath turned into a misty cloud the instant it left her lips. She adjusted the grip on her sword before continuing, a feeling of numbness beginning to creep back into her toes from the icy floor.

Her boot slipped and she adjusted enough to stop a slide. Looking down, she saw the floor was beginning to grow white with frost.

Go no further you foolish girl… this is too dangerous…

She turned to leave, but a shadow cast itself over the opening she'd come in through.

Her boots slid and crunched against the floor as she backed away from the lurking darkness, the thing growing and becoming more human with each passing moment. Turning to look behind her she eyed the broken roof and the roots dangling down.

Run, find the light!

With a burst of speed, she leapt over a pile of debris and began a dead sprint toward the light and snow that drifted in from above. A bone-chilling howl ripped past her from behind, and she felt her bones ache with the call of the tormented voice.

She slipped again on the ice and a billowing darkness fell on her in an instant. She rolled and kicked, razor sharp claws tearing at the leather of her boots, the chill of the attack sending shockwaves of numbing pain up her legs and into her spine.

Her eyes watered, and her boots tangled in the shadow stuff oozing around her like slick oilcloth. She swung her blade against the thing's dark head, and the sword sank against the shadow, frost ripping up the edge and covering her gloved hand.

Another howl split the cold air above her and she caught sight of a second creature. The thing hung from the twisted roots of the tree she'd hoped to use for her escape, its baleful eyes staring into her soul.

She didn't have time to scream, her first attacker striking again, this time drawing three thin lines of blood along her belly as her mail gave way. The blood froze a deep amber color, the chill of the claws icing the flesh and sealing the wounds almost instantly.

She cried out and kicked the thing again, her boots coming free enough for her to slide backward across the slick floor until her helm struck against stone. The ring of metal filled the chamber upon impact. She managed a look up, the stone altar above her sparkling with a golden glow that reached toward the chamber's vault.

The wraith flew at her again, this time ready to drink her fully into its darkness. She forced another roll that took her around the side of the altar, and the creature howled as it pulled up and away. The creature shielded its eyes from the altar's glow, a dark arm flying before its hideous white face.

Above her, the second shadow called to the first, and they circled around to flank her. Without hope, she pushed her legs up under her enough to rise from the floor and look upon the altar-top. The shimmering glow surrounded a gnarled and beautiful staff that lay across a thin-sheathed sword set with a multi-faceted ruby in the pommel.

Reaching her hand inside the glow, her mind was ripped from her body in a blinding flash of images and darkness. Suddenly she was drifting over a half frozen field, her eyes seeing the glint of a mighty wall of ice that stretched from horizon to horizon. Knights rode on huge steeds below her, and at their head was a man in glinting mail with a standard of snow leopard skin flapping in the breeze above his shoulder.

She flew further until she saw the Towers of the Order and the magic beneath them. She waged war with legendary Wizards and sailed the Halo Ocean along the pagan coasts until she found the shores of the Wintertide. There, she witnessed the raising of Castle Sastrine and the founding of the lines of the Ergoroth Queens.

The stream of visions were seen through the eyes of both women and men, until at last she hovered above a single scene, looking down on a woman she didn't recognize. Around her she could see the trappings of a fisherman's home, and as she studied the simple house, a reflection caught her eye. Staring back at her in the smooth surface of a polished bronze plate, was a man… the King of Lystbrook. Although his face was boyish and brash, she could still see the familiar features of the aged and haunted Ergoroth who had raised her under the protective walls of his court.

Before she could see more of him, the image changed back to the woman beneath her. She was on the shores of the coast, her belly swollen and eyes filled with tears. Then the woman was gone and a little whip of a girl appeared, her days spent playing amongst the petty nobles and fishermen until at last she was taken in by the queen just as the images began to slow and finally stopped.

Somewhere inside her she felt magic ripple, like the newly broken surface of a still pond. A woman's haunted voice filled her mind.

"*The spells placed upon the blade and staff are there to keep all interlopers and thieves from touching them, but someone of the ancient bloodlines of the Ergoroth family may take up these arms. Accept this gift, daughter of my daughters...”*

Around her, the room sang with the ringing release of the blade of Sarah, the First Queen of Lystbrook. The ancient queen's black rapier was etched with cold blue runes that marked the entire surface of the ebon relic.

Energy from within the blade's depths helped guide her hand as she struck the mottled white head from the closest wraith. The second undead demon then cowered away, its shadow essence spilling between the crypt vaults until she was once again alone.

The sword hummed, and she stared at the cobalt runes, frost touching the corners of her mouth. Her breath came in great puffs, and she turned toward the door. Leaden legs staggered forth into the fading light of day. Her body ached and her stomach began to bleed as heat returned outside the haunted crypt.

She clutched her torn shirt and covered the wound the best she could before making her way past the newly snow-dusted trees. High above, an owl called in the distance preparing for a night of hunting.

By the time she reached her horse, night had fallen, and she could do little more than pull her bedroll from the saddle and slump into it on the cold and unforgiving path. The blade rested beside her, tired fingers clutching it as the darkness of sleep took her.

Deep in the night she heard words repeating over and over again in her mind, each time a little louder until at last she awoke with a start.

“If you want to live, you must take another's life...”

“Life...” she echoed the voice in her head.

Looking down at the black and azure blade in the false dawn, the runes took on a sapphire glow.

“Now I know why you were so feared ancestor...” she whispered, the wind stealing away her words.

She felt nothing as her mind gradually awakened, at least until she tried to move. Her blanket had collected a fine layer of frost, and underneath it her muscles had tightened into knots and her wounds caked over in dried blood.

The pain was great, as was a gnawing sense of despair. She reached out to grasp the rapier and winced as the movement cracked the newly formed scabs on her belly, causing fresh blood to flow from the wound.

With great effort, she used the sword to stand and saw her horse rear back, shying away from the weapon. She whispered a soothing word to the beast and then hissed a curse as she tried to straighten. More blood dripped down, the laces at her waist growing dark and wet.

A white hue clung to her fingers, each tipped with blue. She tried to move her toes but felt nothing inside her boots.

"If you're there... I can't feel you..." she whispered to her feet.

Pulling a vial of strong alcohol from the bag, she leaned back and cried out as the wounds tore open further and more blood spilled out from her abdomen. Her eyes glazed, and she reached out to find a fallen stick on the ground. Using one hand, she broke the stick and stuck it between her teeth. Clambering backward she felt a tree trunk behind her, and watched through watery eyes as she opened the lid of the vial and poured the liquid across her wounds.

The pain blazed in her mind and she bit and screamed against the stick, but she didn't pass out, the sensation of deep hunger keeping her awake. Looking back at the blade lying on the frozen earth, she couldn't help feeling a need for it.

What are you? She thought.

Forcing her eyes away and back to her purpose, she dropped the vial and found the sewing needle and thread inside the kit. More tears rolled down her cheeks as she touched a lip of tattered flesh under the thick sheen of blood and pierced it with the needle. Panic and pain washed through her as her fingers let go the needle, and she spit out the wood from her mouth.

She began to weep. She could only sit there watching her life pump from her, a greater numbness creeping up her legs.

"*If you want to live...*" the voice in her head hissed.

She cursed and the horse tried to pull away, the reigns holding it fast to a nearby tree.

"I have nothing for you," she whispered between clenched teeth.

"*You must take another's life...*" it said again.

She felt the tears on her cheeks, freezing around her eyes and she smacked her head several times into the bark of the tree behind her, each time letting a curse slip her lips.

Finally, her breath shaking her chest, she opened her eyes and looked at the steed. Her mouth grew dry and she shook her head but she moved anyway, her arms dragging her to the nearby blade.

The horse blew puffs of mist from its nose, eyes black and circling as it fought against the leather that bound it.

If I wait to do this he will go free and I will die...

The blade lay motionless and she felt the final wisps of warmth leaving her fingers.

"If you want to live..."

With a scream she forced her legs under her once more, this time not trying to staunch the flow of blood that flowed down into her boots. She struggled to the sword and found it warm and light beneath her pale fingers. As her hand touched the hilt, an animalistic desire washed over her and she felt the hunger of a thousand years.

Ancient Queen, if this is you driving my hand then make it strike true...

Turning to her horse, rapier in hand, she lunged.

It tried to rear up, but the reins caught it, pulling it down and her strike sliced across its thick neck with the edge of the blade.

Blood gushed forth over the frozen ground and the horse screamed a mournful and twisted cry that sent shivers down her spine. She stumbled away from the falling creature, her eyes on the blade. The blue runes pulsed and the blood that collected on the blade slowly disappeared, the azure glow turning to amber as vapors of *afterglow* slithered around her arm and brought strength to her exhausted body.

As the weapon drank, she felt the warmth increase in her hand until her whole arm began to burn. Her abdomen pulsed and she reached down with trembling fingers to run them over the three jagged wounds.

Blood flowed from the wraith's wound, but she didn't feel the hurt, instead the strength of the horse welled up inside her.

Her dulcet blue eyes flared as she looked from the blade to the horse, the beast falling to its knees before her. A twisted smile washed across her lips and she stepped close, driving the blade tip down into its still warm and rising chest.

With both hands she drove the blade in and fell to her knees beside the creature. Her soul and flesh were bathed with energy from the elemental spark of the beast as the flames of its faltering power were transferred to her in a flare of primordial magic.

The blade feasted, the runes blazing as the horse slowly withered away to a husk upon the snowy ground. She stood, steam rising from her, the blade extended in one hand as she walked back to her bloodstained bedroll and sat. Blood still fell from her wound, but she ignored it, the power of the kill now fully in her grasp.

No chill can claim me, no wound touch my flesh, not with the power of the beast coursing through my veins...

Turning the blade over in her hand she studied it.

The balance was unmatched, the blade a razor's edge, and the black steel turning a rainbow of hues in the sunlight.

"What other gifts can you provide me with?" she asked.

The blade was silent, the will and words of the long dead queen no more.

Looking to the east, she watched the wind blow snow off the skeletal tree limbs.

Sastrine Castle is my home, my blood lives there and I will not be made to run from the rights that are mine...

"I will return to Lystbrook, and there I will set things right," she said.

Walking away from the horse and her equipment, she stomped through the wood, eyes blazing with stolen power.

CHAPTER SIXTEEN

ERIK

I've no time for long talks. If this is what you've come to see, then so be it, but I'll not let your prying eyes distract me now...

Erik turned away from Igrayn's emerald eyes, those orbs raising goose-flesh on his arms. Beyond the party the twin doors loomed up like titans, and he said, "We're going through those doors. I need everyone to keep their wits on a razors edge as we've absolutely no idea what we'll find behind them."

"I'll be of very little help, but what power I have left is yours," Telluria whispered to his right.

She touched him, her fingers like ice against his arm. A shiver went up his spine and his spark guttered in his chest.

"Thank you," Erik replied. He then looked to the priest, "Todmann, please do what you can to keep us fighting."

Todmann bowed. Righting his grip on *Fury*, Erik slowly walked to the entry. The doors loomed up out of the red haze cast by windows that lined the entry hall, the glow whispering of death. Boots clicked against the stone as the rest of them followed, Braxus's breathing heavier than the others as he kept pace.

Erik finally placed a hand on one of the doors and felt nothing but cold metal. He waited a moment with his palm on the surface until he frowned and tipped his head.

"I feel a pulse," he said.

Malcolm stepped forward and placed his hand on the door. Beside him Igrayn followed suit.

"I feel it as well," Malcolm said.

"Could it be the beating of a heart? Could the room somehow be alive?" Erik asked Telluria.

She shook her head, "Living walls do exist, but they're malevolent spirits trapped inside the surface and attack at any opportunity. If this was one of them, you would have already been enveloped."

"Comforting..." Braxus grunted.

Malcolm and Erik both looked at each other before Igrayn broke their silent exchange.

"It is a waltz," Igrayn whispered

"What?" Erik asked.

She turned to look at the two of them, her eyes sparkling like they never had before.

I see the oceanic tropics in you... the light of an endless archipelago and the sun across the water's surface...

"A dance, something found in the courts. I believe it is 'The Morning of Songbirds,'" she answered.

Erik frowned.

I know that song and I always hated dancing to it...

"I really don't like the thoughts going through my head," Malcolm said.

"Whatever the case... everyone better get ready to dance." Erik said.

He leaned his weight into the door. It gave almost immediately, groaning slightly as it swung inward, while a deluge of music poured out into the hall.

The sound of a full orchestra heartily playing "The Morning of Songbirds" resonated from within. Erik raised his weapon, the bright lights from candelabras shining against the red gloom of the dim passageway where the party stood. The throne chamber was illuminated with light and color, a party like the grandest balls in all the north taking place before them.

There must have been three dozen couples in full ball attire drifting across the incredibly polished black and white marble floor. Colorful dresses flowed around lovely ladies, and handsomely dressed men in velvet and silk led a spinning procession of revelers who made no sound other than the rustle of fabric and the shuffle of feet.

No orchestra was visible, and banners of the old Mahe kings decorated the walls. A single jade and gold standard was displayed next to the throne, representing the kingdom of Lystbrook with their majestic kingfisher.

"Skeleton," Malcolm pointed out, his left hand rising toward the throne.

Erik's eyes followed the warrior's finger. Sitting in the seat was a withered corpse wrapped in rotted robes of black trimmed with golden runes, the distinct markings of the Order of Towers. In one of the dead man's hands rested a staff of polished sablewood, topped with twin blades of curved steel. In the other deathly grasp was an object that emitted the same red glow as could be found on the exterior of the palace.

"What of the dancers?" Ash asked.

"They look like they're in a dream," Igrayn said.

Erik looked back at Telluria who gave him an affirmative shake of her head.

"Then I'll try not to wake them," he said.

Turning back to the hall, he slipped among the dancers, his boots scuffing as he dodged around the dancing couples on his way to the throne. Igrayn followed suit, her body gliding through the moving crowd, Tavalori's voice hissing a protest behind her, "Igrayn!", but she never looked back.

Erik smiled inside at the woodman's feeble attempt to stop her.

Foolish boy… she's not yours either and telling her what to do is the worst attack in your already weak arsenal…

By the time Erik made the far side of the room, Igrayn was waiting for him.

"I didn't know you could dance," she said playfully.

"I only do so with the right lady," he shot back.

She watched him a moment, her eyes sparkling with her newfound emerald shine.

"You're not who you say you are either," she replied.

"Is that you or the water goddess talking?" he asked.

She smiled, "I am still myself, Erik. I may have made a bargain for my life with the water goddess that allowed her to change my elemental order, but does that really matter to you?"

He returned the smile, "It matters if you've taken an interest in me at last…"

"You would be wise to keep such bold statements sheathed, sell-sword, as my admirer with a bow might find you a threat and take a shot at you from across the dance floor," she replied.

He never let his eyes leave hers. "What if I don't find him a threat?"

"Then you're not as smart as you pretend to be…"

She turned from him to the throne and Erik bit his lip as his blood raced, his spark firing in his chest.

Damn all the gods that played me…

Following her, he made his way to the dais and stood with her at the foot of the ancient throne, the corpse of a Wizard perched atop it. It was a gaunt thing, wax skin stretched over bone that broke in some places to expose yellow skeleton. The cowl rested low, and the lips were curled back in a kind of grotesque smile, the reek of death somehow still drifting about the corpse in a cloak of vile vapors. The right hand was clutching what looked to be a crystal dagger.

"I don't like that knife," she said.

He nodded. "It looks more like a ceremonial object than an actual weapon."

"Do you see the pulsing?" she asked.

Inside the blade the crimson glow dimmed and flared, pulsing in time with the beat of the waltz.

"I do now…"

"Ok, so Telluria said this Wizard betrayed the royal family," Igrayn said.

"Yes."

She looked back at the circling dancers, "And this party is somehow still going on even after near a thousand years."

Erik looked with her, the waltz continuing in slow circle after slow circle. Each dancer wore a pleasant but unengaged expression, eyes blank as they stared ahead, their bodies moving round and round in perfect form.

Nodding, he said, "She also talked about a demonic pact or something along those lines, which might mean he used this dagger as part of a spell."

Igrayn walked away.

"Hey!" he said.

She didn't react, just continued moving between the dancers, her steps leading her to a large object covered in a golden drape of silk at the far side of the hall.

Following close behind, he whispered, "What are you thinking?"

She didn't react to his words, instead she continued crossing the dance floor until she came to a stop at the far wall, her hand coming up to stroke the folds of the silk drapes there. She grasped hold of the fabric and pulled.

The silk sheath slid to the floor, revealing a platinum-framed oval mirror standing before them.

"Gods..." Erik whispered.

In the reflection, the dancers were no longer contentedly spinning, but silently writhing and screaming as they tore at their own flesh in blind agony. The colorful chamber they'd seen upon entry was a wasteland of tattered fabrics, blood, and decay: and yet they did not die.

Igrayn fell back against Erik's chest in horror, and he held her there a moment before words came to his lips, "Stay strong..."

She pressed against him, her body shaking. He felt a cold spark inside of her somehow. True, her fire no longer burned, but it did not seem entirely gone. It was a strange feeling to be sure, soothing cool and tranquil, but at the same time he didn't want to pull away like he did when he got close to Telluria.

Interesting...

"What kind of damnation is this?" she asked.

"The curse holds more sway than we would have liked to believe, and the Wizard I defeated in the tower must have been some foreign interloper instead of the cause of this nightmare."

She nodded, her hair brushing against his cheek with the scent of a spring rain and flowers carried upon the breeze.

Low water... so different from the salty scent of the high water Wizards...

She spoke again, this time with a hint of concern in her voice, "Erik?"

A smile passed his lips, "Yes?"

He blinked, whatever spell she'd cast on him falling away, as he remembered where they were and why.

"What's on the throne?" she said.

Swinging his right hand out, he touched the frame of the mirror and gently adjusted the angle until the throne came into view.

Igrayn sucked in a sudden breath and backed further into his chest. Sitting on the throne was a man of middling years, wearing fresh spun silken robes, black as midnight and trimmed in gold that spilled around him. He held his staff proudly in his left hand and two baleful green eyes shone brightly as he smiled at them. With his right hand he deftly flipped the crystal dagger over and over again.

A sound hissed through the chamber when he spoke, like rusted metal scraping against stone, "This is a private party, but at least you've brought

me a princess, like I was promised. Such courtesy will surely grant you the boon of a quick death, instead of a place on the dance floor."

Across the hall, Malcolm yelled something that was drowned out by the music, and Braxus began forcing his way through the dancers.

Erik pushed Igrayn roughly to the side, his momentum carrying the two of them away from the mirror as the now standing skeleton raised a boney hand. Blue lightening arched from the throne and shattered the marble floor in the spot they'd just vacated.

"Move!" Erik yelled. The two of them disengaged and scrambled into the milling dancers.

The skeleton turned its creaking head and surveyed the floor from empty eye sockets. Telluria launched a spattering of *afterglow* darts at the creature but the bolts faded even before they touched the rotten fabric on his chest.

The undead mage raised a hand toward the door, a ball of yellow-green fire leaping from it across the room. Tavalori threw himself against Telluria, both of them tumbling out of the direct impact, as the ball of flame shattered the double doors and rained smoking rubble down around the pair.

Erik ducked between a dancing couple, his eyes scanning the milling throng until he saw Igrayn burst forth from the haunted guests beside the throne. Her rapier flashed out, but the Wizard caught her blade with his staff and the ring of the impact chimed amid the music.

The Wizard's dry lips cracked into a smile as he opened his mouth and unleashed a venomous spray of liquid directly at the princess. She sidestepped, but the yellowed fluid splashed along her right arm. A scream tore from her lips as toxic steam rose from the splatter and ate through her clothing.

Elim... you'll pay for that...

Erik stayed with the dancers, Igrayn tearing at her shirt and calling for help, but he maintained concealment, keeping *Fury* raised and ready.

Malcolm appeared from the between the dancers and struck Elim's chest with a bone-cracking blow that shifted the creature's attention from Igrayn toward himself. Malcolm fell back a step, the strike causing no harm to the Wizard, who waved the mercenary away with a skeletal hand. A blast of invisible force struck Malcolm, the impact lifting him from his feet and sending him flying into the dancers.

Like Erik, Braxus must have been waiting for the diversionary attack of his friend before showing himself. As soon as the Wizard struck Malcolm,

Braxus lunged forward from behind a dancing couple and sank his blade all the way to the hilt into Elim's chest. The Wizard turned its skeletal head and opened its jaws attempting the best smile a creature of its kind could muster. Braxus's eyes grew wide as Elim turned his dagger in his right hand and plunged its pulsing crystal blade into the warrior's shoulder.

Erik sprang before the scream had even left Braxus's lips. *Fury* blazing in his hand, he cut downward using all his strength. The blade struck Elim's right forearm and severed the bone with a flash of green sparks.

A raging moan echoed through the room, Elim falling backward with his new stump raised. Braxus collapsed to his knees before the throne, the dagger pulsing in his shoulder and the Wizard's severed hand still clutching the hilt.

"The mirror!" Telluria called from across the room. "The mirror holds the key to the curse and the dagger binds it!"

Erik brought *Fury* down again, but this time the Wizard blocked the blow with his staff.

Braxus staggered to his feet, the left side of his body dragging behind him as he moved toward the mirror. The mercenary dropped his sword and wrapped his right hand around the dead fingers of the Wizard still clinging to the knife.

Elim shrieked again, his staff blazing with blue lightning as he blocked another blow from *Fury* and then turned the weapon at Braxus's back. Erik fell back to shield Braxus but Elim's magic was faster. A bolt of energy shot from the staff and blasted Braxus off his feet, the knife skittering away across the floor amid the dancers.

Two arrows found their mark in the Wizard's chest, ripping through his hollow ribcage and pinning him at and odd angle to the back of the throne.

Thunder boomed, Ash's dragon wand shattering the calm of the music as Elim's staff was blown from his hand with the force of some unseen projectile. Telluria, singed and bloodied, raised a hand and used the same force Elim had against Malcolm to throw three large blocks of the doorframe against the Wizard. They stuck with a sickening impact, Elim's bones cracking under the weight of the projectiles.

The rusted chain voice screamed with rage and shattered the rythmic music in the chamber, Elim spewing hate at all those who opposed him.

"You can't kill me! The dead have no fear of the living!" Elim screamed.

Erik pushed between two twirling couples, his eyes searching the floor until he saw the knife, its pulsing crystal blade glowing amid the feet of dancers close to the mirror. He dove through the cursed souls, slid next to the dagger and snatched it before a booted foot could spin it away from his grasp.

The mirror, it somehow binds this entire thing…

He leapt to his feet and charged the mirror. A blast of *afterglow* shattered the throne and the ruined corpse of Elim rose for the debris with a maniacal laugh.

"Your doom is at hand, thief!" Elim screamed.

The Wizard raised his remaining hand, but Igrayn caught his wrist and pulled his arm down as surge of black energy left his fingers and shattered the marble floor at his feet. Erik didn't look back but dove directly into the mirror, his body tensing for contact.

Instead of tipping or shattering, the mirrored pane bent and gave way, Erik tumbling through to the world on the far side, the screaming corpses now surrounded him. His boots slipped on the bloody floor and the manic howls of demons roared in the darkness around the scene, but the dagger held madness at bay and he stood still among the chaos.

Elim, his body solid and covered with living flesh, watched him from the dais with eyes wide, fear turning the frown lines of his lips.

"Stay back, fool, the dagger will doom us both if you use it here!" Elim cried.

Erik walked forward, Elim shrinking away as he shook his head. Demons laughed and gibbered in strange tongues, Elim's heels brushing the darkness beyond the dais but not daring to move further.

"I will give you eternal life, wealth, power…whatever you will!" Elim pleaded.

Erik kept on, Elim finally straightening up with eyes growing thin.

"Raseri," Erik whispered.

Elim's movements slowed, *afterglow* frozen in a dark cloud around his fingers as the blade's magic played against the passage of time. Erik came on, stepped to the Wizard and then plunged the crystal dagger deep into his heart.

There was a tremor in the magic field about them, and Erik turned and fled. *Fury*'s magic quickly bleeding away: it had been too few hours since he'd last called on its power. Ahead, the dancers turned to ash and the dark walls of the realm closed around the mirror, the far side the only remaining light around him.

He leapt, time quickening around him as the demonic laughter thundered in his ears. The mirror felt like a wall when he hit it, but it gave, shattering out into the real world as he tumbled through onto the hard marble of the ballroom.

Igrayn lay against Tavalori and Malcolm was being helped to his feet by Telluria as Erik felt blood trickling down his cheek. Braxus was near him, and he struggled to crawl across the floor to where his friend lay. When he reached the man, the voices of the others were calling out and he heard Todmann's boots coming across the floor.

Braxus's breath came in shallow gasps, a great pool of blood having formed below him in the minute he'd been in his prone position. Reaching out, Erik took Braxus's hand and wrapped it around the hilt of *Fury* while he whispered the blade's name.

Nothing happened.

"Hold on, helps coming," Erik whispered.

Todmann appeared, knelt, and whispered prayers as he fingered his sunburst symbol, light radiating from his hand.

With a small gasp of air, Braxus took a shuddering breath.

"Am I dead?" He croaked.

"I've given what I can, but only your will can do the rest," Todmann replied.

Braxus was breathing, but he didn't answer and Erik looked at the priest.

"I can't say, his wounds are grievous, and my divine blessings are spent," Todmann said.

Near the throne, Igrayn wept, Tavalori trying to treat her arm but having little skill to do so. The princess whispered between sobs, tears falling from her eyes and her right hand rubbing a silvery pearl necklace at her throat.

"How is he?" Ash asked.

Erik and Todmann turned to look at the Eldaryn, the heat from him almost palpable against their exposed flesh as he stood with ash smudged cheeks and his dragon wand in his hand.

"If we don't get further magic, it doesn't look good," Todmann said.

Ash nodded, "What now?"

Erik shook his head and was about to speak when the sound of boots thumped through the entry hall. Raising *Fury*, he pushed the Eldaryn behind him.

"Be ready," he said.

Ash raised his wand again as a company of tall men in bronze mail, pointed helms and short spears filed into the room. At their breasts they wore tabards the color of the sea and embroidered with twin golden mermaids facing one another.

"Secure this chamber!" barked the rough voice of a man in the lead.

Spearmen moved to circle the party and Erik dropped *Fury* back in its sheath.

"I don't think your wand is needed because if I'm correct we just found our Cursed Legion," Erik said.

Ash lowered the weapon, more soldiers entering through the door.

CHAPTER SEVENTEEN

ERIK

So you've managed to throw my life into another mess, or perhaps divert my river to whatever course most interests you...

I can only say that you reap what you sow, and now that I'm in this you'll have to deal with the consequences.

Whatever the case, it's another unwanted adventure down in my life that just keeps throwing more deadly trials at me. Perhaps that's the cosmic joke, that all I want is good food, warm weather, and lots of beautiful women, but instead I seem to have to work for the meager scraps I get...

Erik sat with the rest of his company, their only conversation having been about how long they were going to be held. He had counted two dozen officers and at least a hundred regular men-at-arms by the time the Legion Commander made his way into the throne anti-chamber.

The commander wore polished half-plate armor and a pressed tabard bore a single mermaid on it, her cheerful face smiling at everyone, as her curvaceous body wrapped around a diamond pointed trident. The man carried his helm under his left arm, and displayed a thick salt and pepper beard on a jutting chin that failed to hide a weathered and battle-scarred face.

When he got to one of the officers, he whispered something and then the subordinate turned to Erik and the others with a thickly accented voice, "The palace is overrun with vermin, and the grounds are unkempt. Not a soul other than the eight of you, including the royal family, is to be found within the walls. My men inform me that a city four times the size of the one that was there yesterday morning now resides outside our gates."

The commander said nothing, but his cool blue eyes scanning those gathered demanding an explanation. The scent of the sea wafted in behind Erik and Igrayn got to her feet.

A scathing eye from the commander stayed her from coming toward the officers, but ever the princess, she held her composure.

"I would explain, if you will allow it?" Igrayn replied coolly.

"And you are?" the subordinate asked.

She straightened even further, the skin along her left arm still bright pink and raw after the cleansing unguents and prayers both she and Todmann had employed.

"I am Igrayn Ergoroth, Princess of Lystbrook," she said.

The commander gave a curse, and then held up his hand to ward her off. "This is not Lystbrook," he said. "And I think you've already caused enough trouble between the king and his court Wizard. I would hear from a fellow countryman."

Igrayn was about to protest when Malcolm pulled her back to her seat and stepped in front of her.

"Ah… well, commander, then I guess you should speak with Sir Erik of Tall Hills," Malcolm said. He gave a slight bow and then waved a blood-crusted hand back toward Erik.

The commander looked to where Erik sat, let his gaze linger on the blade sheathed in his lap and then waved him forward.

"You are a Knight of Aflyr?" the Commander asked.

Erik didn't hesitate, "Yes, Lord Commander, I've been traveling up the Caliper coast these last weeks, skirmishing against Delver uprisings from the Broken Land in the south."

Igrayn pursed her lips but held her tongue, the commander pointing to *Fury*.

"That's no gladius of the Legions," he said.

Erik bowed, "Indeed, but much has changed in the years you've been asleep."

The man scratched his beard. "Go on."

"Let me first start at the beginning, but as haste is needed in all things I'll do my best to be quick. The Court Wizard, Elim, betrayed the king and placed a dark curse on the palace. That magic held you and your legion in some kind of timeless sleep while he played out his revenge on the king and his family."

Men around the commander murmured and he raised a hand to quiet them.

Erik continued, "A thousand years have passed since last you saw the sun rise. Today Aflyr is ruled by a single king and that king sits the throne at his palace in ChanderNagor. As in your time, the eastern king holds no love for Mahe or the western coast, his only concern being for his own safety. Even as we speak, Delvers pour across the middle marches, and the King of Aflyr has moved nearly all this city's garrisons, knights, and noble houses to ChanderNagor in the east. He hopes to sacrifice this city's strength to bolster his own, leaving Mahe to burn without any defense."

"All the garrisons of Mahe?" the commander asked.

"Nearly all. Only boys in armor guard the gates with a skeleton crew. If the city were to be besieged, there would be no hope of holding it. For that reason, I undertook the quest of freeing your now legendary legion. Although the rumors surrounding the curse were vague, I had little choice but to try the one hope left for the city. I knew that only your strength of arms could save this city from total destruction at the hands of the fell invaders," Erik answered.

The commander turned to an officer. "I can't trust such words without verification. Send a company of spears to each of the three city gates to see them secure..." he began, only to be cut short by Erik.

"There are now four gates," Erik interjected.

The man cast him a look before turning back to his subordinate.

"Four companies, four gates. Understood?"

The younger man gave a salute before turning on his heel and leaving the room.

"I greatly hope you're nothing more than a liar and a thief, Sir Erik of Tall Hills, but I cannot so easily dismiss the perils of a Delver invasion," the commander said without turning back to him.

"If what you say is true, then we have a great deal of work ahead, and very little time to do it," he continued. "I'll see that the stocks of healing ointments and restorative scrolls in our barracks are brought to you as well as fresh clothes. But beware, if you are lying, I will make sure you rot in the dungeons."

With a wave to his guards, he left the room and the company breathed a sigh of relief. Erik turned back to Malcolm who gave him a thin smile.

"Sir Erik of Tall Hills?" he whispered.

"Well, it's better than Sir Malcolm of Fishgut Circle," Malcolm replied.

Erik lifted a tankard, the rest of the Company of the Coast, as the townsfolk of Mahe were now calling them, doing the same.

"To a city defended and an adventure worth telling our grandchildren," Erik said.

The others toasted, Braxus gingerly leaning back and taking only a small sip as the rest of the group drank deeply.

"I have to tell you, I was pretty sure none of us would walk out of that palace alive," Malcolm said.

"Hear, hear!" Ash agreed.

The Eldaryn was on a raised stool, the heat from his spark almost canceled by the water of Telluria as she sat next to him. The Wizardress wore white trimmed in gold, the new robes being donned the morning after their release from the palace proper. She also carried Elim's staff, the relic too powerful even for the leadership of the Cursed Legion to want within their ranks.

"Well, I was pretty sure we were going to lose Braxus, but I guess the gods had something else in mind," Erik said.

Braxus nodded, the mercenary's wounds terrible and long to heal even with the city's best magic put to full use on him.

"I'm pretty sure I saw my god more than once in the night after the battle," Braxus said.

"Oh, and did Bandylegs have anything to say?" Ash asked.

The table burst out in laugher, even Telluria joining the mirth, and Erik leaned back and watched them all. Tavalori sat next to Igrayn, the princess leaning close to the young man, but she didn't touch him like she had in the past.

Ash and Braxus were the young couples constant companions during the four days since their release from the palace, and Malcolm had spent his days helping bolster the defense of the gates as a new legion inductee. Todmann drank with them as well, a froth of foam on his mustache and a glimmer of light in his eyes even though two of his order had been found dead inside the healing room where Erik had left Raziel the week before and the bodyguard mysteriously gone.

"With such great success, what new adventure awaits us next?" Ash asked.

"New adventure? Don't you think we've had enough for one lifetime?" Todmann asked.

"I'm not so sure adventure is in our cards, my fiery friend, but certainly this Delver menace isn't at an end so that should keep at least a few of us busy in the coming weeks," Erik said.

"And you think you'll be doing something about that?" Igrayn asked.

Erik looked at her, unable to stop the hint of a smile on his lips, "As a Knight of Aflyr, it's my duty."

She rolled her eyes, and the table laughed again, even Braxus.

"Just because Malcolm is quick on his feet with a well-timed lie doesn't make you noble," she said.

"And being born into royalty doesn't make you noble either," he replied.

Eyes were raised around the table, and the smell of the sea rolled in.

Damn, I shouldn't have said that...

"I should march right up to the palace and tell them the truth," Igrayn said.

"Be sure to add that you've no bodyguard left to you here in the city and that by all rights you should be trussed up and sent back to Lystbrook for safe keeping," Erik added.

They stared at each other a long moment until Tavalori put his hand on Igrayn's but she pulled hers away, breaking eye contact.

"I'll be glad to be rid of one of this company at least," she said.

Erik rose, "On that note..."

"Erik, don't go, we've just begun to celebrate," Ash said.

"Yes, let's not end the night on a note like this," Telluria added.

Erik shook his head, and Igrayn avoided his eyes and took a drink from her tankard. "No, I've got business to attend and the sea is too strong in this place tonight."

There were a few more pleas, but he bowed out and exited the tavern, the cool night air harsh on his lungs. Before he'd taken three steps a man appeared, his livery marking him as a page from the legion.

"The Lord Commander wishes to see you," he said, walking over and handing Erik the reins of his horse.

"At this hour?" Erik asked.

"Those were the orders given."

Erik nodded and mounted the saddle, "Very well."

A mist had blown in off the water, and it took them the greater part of the ride to leave it behind, at last rising up on the palace hill with the Ghost Moon coming into view. The palace was lit with white light and looked like an island among the clouds as they came up the rounded road that led to the main gate. Off to the southeast, the Temple of the Sun rose above the mists as well, flame lighting the Temple Hill. Both the palace and temple complexes seemed to signal one another from across the white sea of mist.

"A beautiful evening," Erik said.

The page remained quiet, only his horse's hooves making sound. Once through the gatehouse they made their way around to the upper palace and dismounted, grooms taking their horses. Erik removed his helm and tossed it to a squire. His steps brisk, he made his way to the Regent's entry past two spear-wielding guards. His boots sounded in the hollow hall, the well-lit audience chamber reserved for the King's Regent, but now occupied by Legion Commander Maxus.

The older man turned to greet Erik, his attention drawn away from a sub-commander who was showing him a scroll.

"Sir Erik," Maxus called.

"Legion Commander," Erik replied, giving the man a slight bow.

The grizzled veteran bade him have a seat at a round table newly brought to the room. Both men sat, Erik undoing his sword-belt and laying *Fury* across the table.

"I've been told the inspections are completed and you believe the city secure, although you missed your last appointed briefing time," Maxus said.

Erik frowned but didn't turn back to where his page stood. "Yes, I had other business to attend. The Master of Trades needed to see me."

The man raised an eyebrow, "I had no idea the Master of Trades was still within the city."

"Truly, he's not, but his daughter is here in his stead seeking the ship *Westerly Traveler*. She wanted to be sure the docks were secure and that her cargo would reach her father's warehouses intact."

"And you assuaged her fears?" Maxus smiled.

"Indeed."

"Very well, then one matter is settled, but I fear the second will not be as easy," Maxus began. "My outriders and lancers have confirmed what you feared. The enemy is indeed along the coasts and even raiding farms inland. However, the scouts could find no sign of an army, but Delver bands are having a field day with local communities and outlying farms."

"Do you have numbers?" Erik asked.

"Several thousand Delvers and at least five full army cohorts of Jai-Ruks leading them."

"Without you, Mahe couldn't stand against those numbers," Erik said.

Maxus nodded, "True, but the western coast needs protection as well as the city, and unless we find what's happened to Nehru Fortress I can't spare many men away from these walls."

"Meaning?" Erik asked.

Maxus gave a wan smile, "Meaning, I want to test your metal and devotion once more. If you be a true Knight of Aflyr, then I'll charge you with going to Nehru and finding its fate."

"And what of ChanderNagor?" Erik asked.

Maxus's face grew dark. "What of it?"

"I see, and how many will I be given?" Erik asked.

"I can spare 500 lances, which won't do me good defending walls anyway," Maxus said.

"Malcolm?"

"Yours if you need him."

"I'd also like to take my company, as they've served me well and we have a history against these Delvers in the south," Erik said.

"I see no reason why not, but there is still the matter of the Lystbrook princess," Maxus said.

"Legally, we have no say over her comings and goings, but I will take her under my shield if her safety is a concern," Erik offered.

Maxus raised a brow, "And why would you do something like that?"

"I'm a knight, she's a princess," Erik said.

"You make it sound like a children's tale and not the weighty political situation it is," Maxus said.

"True, but I think there's more to her story than she's letting on, probably something more to do with Aflyr, and only if I keep her close might I discover it," Erik said.

Maxus sighed and crossed his arms over his chest, "That's a dangerous game."

"These are dangerous times, and as you've no deep loyalty to any power that resides outside Mahe, then I say we take what chance provides," Erik said.

"Very well, the princess can go with you, as can the others, but be warned, my outriders say the roads to ChanderNagor are garrisoned at the Joanna River, and the winter fast approaches."

Erik nodded, got to his feet and took his blade.

"May the spirits of the sea go with you," Maxus said.

"And may the spirits of fire give you strength," Erik replied.

Erik got to the door before Maxus cleared his throat. Erik paused, hand on the handle, and Maxus spoke, "Sir Erik, one last thing."

Erik turned back, "Yes?"

"I'm a military man and have not an ounce of noble blood within me. I was charged by my long dead king to see to the defense of his kingdom, which now is only a small portion of a much larger kingdom. I lead men, not countries. These people need someone to look up to, a figurehead with the blood of their own in his veins. Do you understand what I am saying?"

Erik nodded, "I do."

Maxus sighed, "Then do this; protect the people, and when you return I'll see to it that my legion understands who they truly work for."

Erik saluted the commander with a quick strike of his arm across his chest.

An interesting turn… and one with so many possibilities…

Turning on his heel, he left the hall, Maxus barking out further orders to his sub-commanders in the room beyond.

CHAPTER EIGHTEEN

RELAN

Do you believe I'm outside the bounds of my responsibility? I know it's a question that lurks within your mind, the tendrils of it washing against my thoughts like waves against the shore.

Perhaps you're right, but I will make this journey nonetheless, and when it is done you can set your final judgment upon me and I will accept the verdict without plea or retort.

The shadow of death now resides on my hands, the stain untenable unless I find a purpose to it greater than the loss of half a hundred trees. That is my way, and I must keep to my convictions or be lost inside the maelstrom of guilt for the remainder of my days...

Relan walked among the skeletal trees, the mid-winter sun shallow and pale in the sky.

He looked up, a cold southern breeze playing among the brown tangles of the forest, the deeper snowline he'd created the day before left far behind to the northeast.

No bird-form for me now... my powers diminished from the summoning and the leagues ahead must once again be travelled on feet already weary from the former journey...

The eastern foothills of the Wintertide were a tangle of thickets, minor glens, and scattered homesteads as the small kingdom of Lystbrook pressed its domain ever further into the realms of nature.

The horse track of a logger's trail, the path old and ill-kept, held his course toward humanity for an hour before he found a healthy stand of young growth among a graveyard of stumps.

Nature recovers, assuming the humans are wise enough to let it...

Near the western edge of the clearing a small cabin stood half-tumbled down on itself and two saplings sprouted out of its shattered roof.

Making his way to the collapsed dwelling, he slipped inside, cleared bits of debris, and nestled down amid several season's worth of dead leaves. The air smelled of rot, and the floor was damp and cold. Relan waved his staff over the leaves as a prayer whispered from his lips.

"Oak Father, bless this bed that it might greet me with all the warmth and comfort nature can provide."

The trio of twisting firebirds on the staff's head glowed, heat radiating out as the mash of leaves turned from deep brown to the color of desert sand, the edges of the leaves twisting up as the water was drawn from them.

Laying his staff aside, he drew forth a bag from his belt and worked the leather knot, his fingers pulling and pressing until he stopped suddenly.

He lifted his head, sniffed the air, and the crisp sound of a snap drifted through the open roof. Reaching out, he took up the staff again and dropped the bag, eyes scanning through the holes in the logs of the cabin wall.

Beyond his cover, the young forest was a grey collection of skeletons amid the thin layer of snow. His breathing was shallow and he moved along the wall until he caught a bit of movement coming through the trees.

Human...

A woman appeared, cloaked in blue, helmed, and covered in blood from her boots to gloves.

How can she still be walking with that much blood on her... unless, of course, it's not her own?

He watched as she continued on through the trees, her feet slowly kicking up snow as she made her way to the cabin. When she was within twenty feet, he stepped from the broken door, staff held forward.

"Hold interloper! Do not approach any further," he said.

She looked up, the beauty of youth playing across her pale face and cut features. With eyes colored like a tranquil ocean, the woman blinked and then she staggered one more step before she fell to a knee.

He watched her, his staff still held at the ready. Shining mail twinkled in the daylight beneath the folds of her cloak and the hilt of a jewel-studded sword played at her hip.

"There is no place for a knight among the boughs of the Wintertide," he said.

She shook her head, eyes downcast, whispering, "I'm no knight..."

"Then you are regally equipped for a brigand or wayfarer," Relan said.

"Please... I must find the king... something vile is afoot and I must..." she trailed off.

Relan tilted his head, the woman's breathing growing ragged until she slumped forward into the snow.

He watched her a moment, walked forward and prodded her with his staff. She made little noise and he gave a long sigh.

What test is this, a Corsair among the wood and one marked with the livery of Lystbrook. She might be a messenger from the frozen army, but I doubt one would have been sent before my magic sealed them in their wintery tomb, or for that matter be traveling from the south instead of the north...

He pushed her over, the helm tumbling off her head to expose a long mane of brown hair touched with copper. Her scale shirt had been torn at the stomach, three deep slashes, a terrible wound still seeping blood.

Nothing should have survived such a blow for long, and she looks to have come a long distance on foot. Magic is certainly at work... the stink of water is in the air as is the reek of afterglow magic...

She stirred, eyes opening a moment before closing again and Relan looked from her back to the cabin.

"I'm sure to regret this, but as I've already involved myself in the affairs of the outside world I must stay the course," he said.

He waved a hand over her, "Roots beneath, come alive."

The snow trembled and leaves burst forth with a tangle of twitching roots. The young woman was lifted from the snow and he waved her on, the roots staying beneath her as they passed her weight along until she entered the cabin.

There, he rapped the staff on the earth and the phoenix trio burst into light, warmth filling the chamber. He retrieved his bag, worked the tether, and brought forth a poultice from one of the many pouches.

"It will be the last of my blessings, and the healing must come from your own spirit as much as the natural salves and power of the Oak Father, but if you've come this far then perhaps there is a reason inside that you will survive this night to see the dawn." he whispered.

She murmured again, and he applied the poultice to the wound, his fingers working the green mush into the flesh as he prayed to the Oak Father to bring power to the healing inside the already potent salve. When it was done, he settled in, his staff across this lap and the light from the tip glowing golden in the coming night.

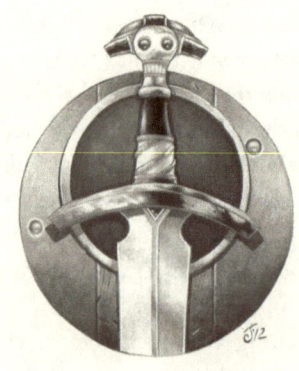

Author Scott Taylor has worked as a writer and editor of both fantasy and science fiction for the past decade and is currently the Senior Editor for Black Gate Books, a blogger for Black Gate Magazine's Website, and the founder of Art of the Genre Publishing. He lives in Ranchos Palos Verdes, California with his wife and son where he enjoys practicing a Peter Pan lifestyle.

Artist Jeff Easley is perhaps the greatest fantasy painter of the modern age. He has spent the past 30 years defining fantasy in works like Dungeons & Dragons, countless novels, Magic the Gathering, and all other manner of fantasy and science fiction art. He currently resides in Lake Geneva, Wisconsin.

www.ingramcontent.com/pod-product-compliance
Lightning Source LLC
Chambersburg PA
CBHW051918240626
47153CB00004B/1271